She turned and looked me full in the eye. I gathered my courage and took a step toward her. "What do you say we find out if you're a lesbian?"

She backed up against the table, her cheeks reddening, as I closed the distance between us. Leaning into her, I inhaled her breath, beery and warm. I heard her swift intake of air as I touched her lips with mine. Her mouth crumpled softly.

I wanted to sustain that first kiss, always so exciting and filled with promise, but I noticed her eyes slewing sideways toward the windows and doors. I released her. "Are you expecting someone?"

"No. It's just that everything is so open. Let's lower the blinds."

Feeling a stab of excitement, I hurried around with her to let the blinds down. She locked the doors. Then we stood in the middle of the room, looking at each other.

"Which is your bed?" I asked, when she seemed struck speechless.

Visit

Bella Books

at

BellaBooks.com

or call our toll-free number
1-800-729-4992

Abby's Passion

Jackie Calhoun

Bella
BOOKS
2005

Bella Books, Inc.
P.O. Box 10543
Tallahassee, FL 32302

Printed in the United States of America on acid-free paper
First Edition

Editor: Anna Chinappi
Cover designer: Sandy Knowles

ISBN 1-59493-014-7

*This work of fiction is dedicated to Diane Mandler,
my live-in social worker.*

Acknowledging:

Anna Chinappi, my editor, a great person to work with.
Diane Mandler, for her knowledge and insight.
Joan Hendry and Chris Calhoun, my first proofreaders.
Sandy Schmeck for commentary.

Thanks also to Linda Hill, Terese, and the others at Bella
Books for doing their jobs so well.

I

Lisa, my ex, once asked me, "What's your passion, Abby, because it sure isn't me." I'd laughed, but the question had set me wondering. Was it my clients? My work? I'd told her I had more than one passion—her, good fiction, water, woods, wildlife. Not my clients, though; for them I had compassion.

In the rearview mirror, I looked every bit of forty-two, which I was. I hadn't slept well the previous night. Nothing unusual. I often had trouble falling asleep, and when I woke in the night, I sometimes stayed that way for hours.

Thin red lines streaked like spokes away from the dark blue centers of my eyes. Baring my teeth, I ran my tongue over them in a futile effort to wipe away lunch. My hair, thick and short and wavy, was laced with coarse gray strands that had snuck in among the black. In contrast, my face was winter white.

A few days of sun and above freezing temperatures had melted some of the little and now very dirty snow we'd had, exposing clumps of earth, dead grass, dog turds, cigarettes. Yet winter hadn't released its grip. No wonder so many people were coming up on call.

I found a parking slot outside the hospital, doused my eyes with drops, and went sniffling in through the emergency entrance.

Jennifer, one of the admitting personnel, jerked her head toward the swinging doors to the emergency room. "He's already in there, Abby." As a psychiatric social worker for county mental health services, I'd been here so many times that I knew most of the staff and they knew me.

On the other side of the doors one of the nurses, Carol Watkins, took me into the curtained cubicle where Karl Jankowski sat on a gurney, chin sunk on his chest. He stank of vomit, liquor, and cigarettes. It both annoyed and saddened me to look at him. He'd thrown away everything—wife, kids, home—for alcohol. The guy was a great mechanic, but he'd been fired time and again. He was probably looking for a warm bed and some free food.

"What's the story?" I asked Carol.

"He got into a fight in a bar. Then he jabbed himself with a pocket knife in the back of the squad car." So he could claim to be suicidal and be taken to the hospital rather than jail, no doubt.

Karl showed up rather often in ER. Treatment washed off him like water and, of course, he never followed through with the threatened suicide. There wasn't much sense talking to him when he was under the influence, but that was my job.

"What's up, Karl?"

His chin rose, then fell again. Drops of dried blood stained his pants and shirt. He wasn't a bad looking guy, although the alcohol had left its mark. He mumbled, "I'd be better off dead."

How many drunks had mouthed those words and then forgot them after they sobered up? "You'll feel better tomorrow."

I went outside the cubicle to talk to the doctor in charge and the policemen who'd brought Karl in.

"This is a guy who keeps showing up in ER, who has been through treatment so many times he could teach the class," I said. "Give him a wake-up call. Put him in jail till he sobers up."

Neither the police nor the doctor wanted the responsibility for Karl. "Why don't we admit him overnight?" the doctor said.

"Because it costs the county a bundle and it's just what he wants. In a few weeks he'll be back again, never having come in for any follow-up."

"What if he's serious about the suicide thing?" one of the policemen asked.

"Take his clothes away," I said. "Put him in one of those canvas outfits."

"Okay," the cop said suddenly. "We'll put him in jail."

The doctor waived responsibility. For once they were actually listening to me, instead of trying to cover their asses. My beeper sounded, and I went outside to call work.

"Remember Anna Pagent, the lady who showed up in court in her pajamas and bathrobe and slippers?" asked Sarah Moran, her voice gruff from years of smoking. As one of the phone workers, Sarah was trained to know when to counsel and when to hand a case over to mental health workers like me.

"How could I forget?" Anna had thought she was wearing a pink pantsuit with matching shoes. Her appearance had helped convince the judge she needed to be under county supervision. We'd put her in the hospital for a week to be stabilized and then handed her over to case management.

"Tracy says she's not taking her meds. The police are bringing her to the hospital." Tracy Abbot was Anna's case manager.

"I'll hang around." While I waited, I filled out papers in the lobby.

As the police escorted Karl out the door, he lifted his head and muttered something like, "Want to stay here," and I briefly second-guessed myself. Maybe I should have had him admitted.

It was past four-thirty, too late to return to the office. I went back to the ER to tell them the police were on their way with Anna moments before she appeared.

She came through the doors on the arms of the cops, her feet barely touching the floor. "They're trying to poison me," she

3

hollered as she shook off the policemen. She wore a pair of ragged coveralls crammed into overshoes. Her defiance in facing what she perceived as a real threat wrenched my heart.

Her faded blue eyes, her soft, crumpled skin, her hair floating around her head in a white halo gave her a fragile appearance. But then she twisted her mouth and spat, "Scrawny bitch. You put me away."

I backed up a step. I had been the one who authorized her stay in the hospital last time. "How are you, Anna?"

"Ms. Pagent to you," she snapped. "I want to go home. They're trying to kill me."

I ushered her into one of the cubicles and drew the curtain shut. "Who's trying to kill you, Anna?"

"They'll make me take poison pills with poison water." She looked past me, eyes wild, scared, convinced she was about to be murdered.

"They won't make you take anything against your will, Anna. I promise. Tracy will be in to see you tomorrow." I patted her hand, wanting to reassure her, but she snatched it away. "They'll take good care of you here," I added. Knowing I couldn't convince her of that, I felt as helpless as she probably did.

Outside the cubicle, I talked softly to the doctor.

"Don't listen to that bony bitch. She wants to lock me up," Anna shouted. "Why can't I go home? I have my rights. I'm an American citizen, not a terrorist."

The doctor and nurse went in to calm her. Later the staff would take Anna upstairs to the psychiatric unit and coax her back on her medication.

"Crazy as a bedbug," muttered a guy on his way to a cubicle.

Of course, she was crazy. She was schizophrenic and off her meds. Karl was pathetic, a product largely of his own making. But Anna was the victim of a brain disorder. I had to distance myself from emotional involvement with clients, or I'd be of no use to them. At times I worried that I'd end up without feeling, unemotional, as if I were schizophrenic myself.

Back in the car, listening to *All Things Considered* almost made ending things seem a sane consideration. The world at risk, the environment imperiled, the stock market on a downhill spiral. I'd never be able to retire.

I sometimes thought I should have gotten my degrees in business or journalism, both of which I considered, rather than social work. Would I be happier, more secure? We were so busy at work, we didn't have enough time for our clients. Meetings for everything from staffing to planning emergency contingencies in case of a terrorist attack took many hours of the week. Yet we went about business as usual as if our jobs were safe and we were indispensable, when, in fact, the state-mandated services we provided would evaporate without the necessary funding. Mental health needs hovered near the bottom of the list of essential services. Our clients were forgotten people.

At the grocery store, I ran into Nance Longworth in the bread aisle and greeted her, "Hey, girlfriend, how are you? Thirsty? Hungry? I'm unattached and both."

Nance was my oldest friend, going back to sixth grade. "Where's Dennis?" I asked.

"Having dinner with some work-related person. Let's go to the wine bar. You look like you could use some cheering up."

"Do I? It's just the news, my job, my life. I'll have to call Mona." Fishing my cell phone out of my purse, I placed the call.

Mona answered breathlessly, immediately, "Hello."

"It's only me," I said. I would have asked what she was up to, but decided I didn't want to know. "I ran into Nance in the store. I'm going to be a little late. Go ahead and eat. There are leftovers in the fridge. Call my cell phone number if you need me."

"I could meet you."

"It'll take too long. I've got to go." I felt guilty as I put the phone back in my purse, but I saw more than enough of Mona.

The wine bar was small, cozy, and offered good food. Nance and I sat at the bar, nursing glasses of pinot grigio.

"How is Mona?" she asked.

"The same." I never knew what I'd come home to. Once she'd painted the foyer dark red. It was like walking into an artery. Fortunately, we seldom used the front door.

We moved to an empty table. I ordered salmon. Nance chose shrimp scampi. The waitress brought us each another glass of wine and a basket of bread. When she left, I asked, "Why didn't you go to dinner with Dennis?"

"He didn't invite me." Nance had put on weight over the years. She was still a good-looking woman, though, bottle blonde with snapping brown eyes and magnificent breasts. Smart too, with a master's degree in business. She was one of the most successful real estate agents around.

"If it's business, I suppose you'd be bored." I used Nance and Dennis's home for a bed when I was on call overnight and weekends. One of my weekends was coming up.

She shrugged. "That's why I didn't go. How's work?"

"Am I scrawny or bony, Nance? Tell me the truth."

She laughed. "Where did that come from?"

"A client."

"I wish I were as skinny," she said.

I thought *slender* would be a better word.

It was dark when I got home. Our parents had turned their property—two acres with a house and outbuildings—over to us for safekeeping when they retired to Arizona three years ago. I parked in front of the attached two-car garage and walked toward the back door. The outside light put out a feeble glow against a sky dark with clouds, making me think I should have movement sensor lights installed on the garage, especially since one of us had to park outside. The yard mower, snowblower, and extra fridge took up too much space.

Something glinted on the walk. When I bent over to see it better, an object zipped past my shoulder, followed immediately by a heart-rending crack. I dove behind the yews that lined the walkway.

Our dad had taught us to shoot when we were kids. Mona was pretty good at it. When she was stabilized, she was fairly predictable. I wondered if she'd been slacking off her medications. She liked the highs. I thought of Anna, so mistakenly sure that strangers were intent on poisoning her. Here was my own sister trying to kill me. Or maybe she was just mad at me for not inviting her to join Nance and me for dinner.

Another shot rang out. I jumped. "Mona, it's me. Abby," I yelled toward the garden. Faint lights glimmered from candles set in cans on posts. It wasn't unusual for Mona to practice shooting, even at night, but the bullets were zinging in the wrong direction.

She walked to the edge of the garden. The rifle hung in the crook of her arm. "Why didn't you say so?"

"Put the gun down."

She set the gun against a post and peered into the dark. "Why are you sneaking around?"

"Step away from it," I yelled, mad as hell.

She did.

I came out from behind the bushes, every muscle tense.

"I was practicing my night aim and thought someone was trying to break in."

Grabbing the rifle, I emptied the chambers and put the bullets in my pockets.

"Dad gave me that gun. Give it back," she said, holding a hand out for it.

I stared at her. Her reddish-brown tinted hair curled wildly around her face. The black of her pupils had taken over the dark blue irises, so like my own, and they were now encircled by the whites. She looked dangerous.

"No way. You damn near killed me." The anger began to ebb.

"Don't take it away," she whined. "It's all I've got left of Daddy."

"You've got the house and everything in it that belonged to Mom and Dad. You talk like they're dead."

"They may as well be. They ran away from me." Her face crumpled a little.

"No, they didn't," I said, although I sometimes wondered if they had. "If you kill someone, though, you'll end up in jail."

"I've got a good lawyer," she countered. These seven years she'd worked part-time for a woman attorney in town, Sally Shields, one of her high school friends.

"And what if you'd shot me?"

"I'm sorry, Abby," she said contritely. "Someone robbed the Kwik Trip yesterday."

I gestured around us. "Look at this place. No one in their right mind would think to rob us."

"I said I'm sorry."

"Let's go inside, Mona."

II

Mona's husband had left her seven years ago, which was when she'd returned home. Then Mom and Dad went south and asked me to move into the house with Mona. My partner at the time had agreed, but it soon became apparent that Mona was more than Lisa had bargained for. Lisa had packed her bags when Mona drew a mural of naked women on our bedroom wall.

Occasionally, I'd bring someone home. Always a mistake. Mona would prepare elaborate dinners with five courses, more than three people could put away, deck out the house with vases of flowers, and overwhelm the guest with talk. She'd stick around, dominating the conversation, till the woman fled. Then she'd feel terrible for driving off my date, but we'd go through the same scenario the next time.

"Want to play cribbage?" she asked. She'd made popcorn, bowls of it, enough for five people.

"Okay," I said, although I wanted nothing more than to climb into bed with a book. I knew she was lonely. She'd scared off most of her friends.

"I called Douglas today," she said as she dealt the cards. We kept a running score of games won and lost.

Her ex-husband. "Why?"

"It's our wedding anniversary."

"That's right." I remembered. "What did he have to say?"

"He was out of town or so his secretary said."

I knew Douglas wanted nothing to do with her. He'd told me so. I pegged two points on a pair before she jumped up, grabbed a handful of popcorn, and began to pace. The kernels fell through her fingers onto the carpet.

"Your turn," I said.

"I think we should add a sunporch." She slapped down another card to make three of a kind, pegging six points. Then she was on her feet again.

"Too much money," I said automatically. Living with her was like working all the time. "Have you been taking your meds, Mona?"

"I hate taking pills," she countered. "I'm all right. Think how good the sun would feel when it's cold and gray out like today."

"Take your meds," I said, throwing down the cards and heading toward the kitchen.

She followed, still on a roll about adding a sunporch.

We'd updated the kitchen a few years ago, putting in a built-in dishwasher, modern fridge, a new stove and sink. We'd had the floor redone in large ceramic tiles and the pine cupboards refinished. The strip for her pills lay by the sink. It was empty.

I tapped the container on the counter. "Where are they?"

"I took them all." She gave me a stubborn look. Arms crossed, head back, mouth straight.

I sighed. "Do you want to crash or worse, Mona?" I didn't know which was worse, actually. A deep depression or severe mania. Either could land her in the hospital.

"I won't."

I studied her for a moment. She grew more agitated. Going to my room, I found the pills I'd hidden from her. I made her take the day's dosage and refilled her strip. Tomorrow I'd pick up a refill at the pharmacy.

"Swallow, Mona. *Now.*"

She did, then opened her mouth for me to see that she had. I hated this. I hadn't grown up to be my sister's caretaker.

It took a while to finish the game with her jumping up, pacing and talking between turns. I went to my room exhausted. The bed lamp cast shadows on the naked women adorning the wall. I hadn't painted over them or asked Mona to do so, because I kind of liked them.

Mona knocked and came in as I pulled a sleep shirt over my head. "I picked up some brochures for the sunporch," she said as if we'd decided on the addition and just needed to make a selection.

"Where'd you get them?" I'd have to call and put a stop to anything that might be in the works if I didn't want to come home someday and find the sunporch in place.

"Sun Sensations. They do hot tubs too. Wouldn't that be nice on a sunporch? Let me show you the pictures." She spread on my bed the pamphlets with the glassed-in enclosures and hot tubs.

Mona wasn't just a dreamer. When she got an idea, she put it into effect whether there was money for it or not. Once she bought three vehicles without consulting Douglas—a Mustang, an Explorer, and a Ranger pickup. She said she'd covered all contingencies. Douglas had told me that's when he decided to leave her.

"Why don't you just paint the inside of the house? That would be a big improvement."

"What colors do you think?"

"Whites and off-whites. Not my bedroom, though, or the kitchen or bathroom." The naked ladies were on my wall and the other two rooms had been done. "The place is dreary." The living room and dining room walls were a dull peach color, left over from our parents' days.

"Boring, but I'll see what we've got."

"Whatever we have is old. Why don't we look at samples over the weekend?" When her meds took hold, she wouldn't have so much energy. I just hoped she wouldn't crash or go severely manic before they did. I dealt with depression on a day-to-day basis. Mona's ranked among the worst.

"Okay." She headed toward the door.

"What are you going to do now?" I asked wearily.

"Clean." She seldom slept when she was manic.

I fell asleep to the sound of the vacuum cleaner running downstairs and awakened to *Morning Edition* on public radio. My eyes were drawn to the naked women in the light of day. Two were kissing and fondling each other. No wonder Lisa had been so startled, although I think it was the invasion of our privacy that had alarmed her most. I was used to it. Mona had been in my face since she became old enough to walk and talk. I was the elder by four years. Our brother, Craig, had been born in the interval.

Stretching, I thought about the day ahead of me. After staffing, I had clients scheduled every hour. Getting up, I headed for the shower. The house was silent. Knowing that Mona had to get ready for work, I tapped on her door. No answer. I stuck my head in the opening. She was buried under the covers, the shades drawn against the daylight. I'd wake her after my shower.

The upstairs bathroom had been modernized when the work on the kitchen was done. We'd had an enclosure with doors installed around the tub/shower. A pedestal sink had been put in and a water-saving toilet. The floor had been redone in ceramic tiles, the walls repaired and repainted. A fan, heating lamp, and regular light were encased overhead. A window overlooked the backyard.

I glanced out at the dead grass and leaves and tall stalks in the garden and the tin cans. Most were lying in the garden with holes in them. At least five doves stood in a pile of sunflower seeds on the platform feeder with one bright red cardinal among them. Goldfinches, still in winter garb, perched on the tube feeders. A chickadee chased off a goldfinch and fluttered onto its perch.

The bathroom door opened as I stood under the warm shower, working shampoo into my hair. Knowing it was Mona, I wondered apprehensively why she hadn't said anything. Chancing a look, I saw her sitting on the john, her forearms on her thighs, her head hanging between her shoulders. Shit, I thought. The medicine hadn't gotten to her in time. She'd slid into depression.

She was still sitting when I stepped out of the tub. I sighed. "Are you going to work?"

She nodded. Her employer had stood by her through highs and lows. When Mona couldn't work, Sally hired someone from a temporary agency. I was grateful to her.

Drying off, I felt tired already. Mona's depressions affected me, too. "Come on, get in the shower. I'll fix breakfast. We need to get some medication into you."

She stood as if she carried a yoke on her shoulders and slumped toward the tub, shedding her pajamas as she went. I found myself irritated by her demeanor, by her unwillingness to take her meds till it was too late. If Anna lived alone, so could Mona. I angrily shut the door behind me with more force than necessary.

Mona ate the oatmeal I made for us, the toast I buttered. She was dressed sloppily, her hair carelessly brushed, no makeup or jewelry. Normally, Mona took pride in her appearance. Where I put on little more than sunblock and chapstick, she carefully made up her face. Her dangling earrings were her trademark, her clothes fashionable. I liked my shoes clean and whatever I wore pressed, but I paid little attention to what was in vogue. I watched her swallow her medications without protest. Her listlessness finally twisted my heart toward sympathy.

I called Sally from work while my computer booted up. Sally had done her undergraduate work and earned her law degree at University of Wisconsin-Madison. Mona had gone to the University of Wisconsin-Oshkosh. She'd married Douglas in her senior year and followed him to Marquette where he became a dentist and she presented her first diagnosable symptoms of bipolar disorder. I'd already completed my undergraduate and graduate studies at the University of Wisconsin-Madison and was working for the county.

Sally picked up. "Hi, Abby. Mona's here. Barely. What happened?"

"She wasn't taking her meds. She is now. If she goes home, give me a buzz, will you? I'll be in all day, except during the noon hour." I walked on my lunch hour. It was how I kept my sanity and waistline.

"Will do. We'll keep an eye on her." Sally had a partner, a receptionist, and two full-time assistants besides Mona.

"Thanks." I didn't like Mona to be alone when she fell into one of her depressions. Suicide and depression were closely linked.

I called Sun Sensations and told them my name would have to be on any contract Mona signed regarding the property. After that, I read my e-mail, notified Anna's case manager of her hospitalization, and went to the tiny kitchen to pour a cup of coffee before staffing. Someone had brought in a box of doughnut holes. At work, food disappeared almost as soon as it appeared.

My mouth was full when my boss, Sylvia Peters, came in and poured herself coffee. She began talking about her youngest child, who was about to graduate from high school and wanted to join the military. I couldn't blame her for being upset. The girl had been accepted at Northwestern University. We were walking toward the phone room where the crisis unit staffed in the mornings, when Sylvia ducked into her office to catch a phone call. During staff meetings, we met to discuss the cases that had come up on call, assign those cases as needed, brainstorm ideas that might help us with our own clients, and drink a lot of coffee.

Four of us made up the crisis team—me, Mark, Bob, and Debbie. The others looked up when I entered. I considered them as much friends as co-workers. Mark had been on call the night before and looked beat.

"Busy night?" I asked.

"From midnight on ER was jumping."

"You look it."

"I feel it," he said dryly.

"Have any of you thought about adding a sunporch?" I asked.

"We have," Bob said.

"You're going to add a sunporch?" Debbie asked.

"Mona wants one."

"How is she?" Mark asked.

"She tried to kill me last night. She was target shooting and thought I was an intruder."

"She's a pretty good shot, isn't she?" Mark looked less tired and more interested.

"Better than I am."

"And what did you do?" Debbie asked.

"Dove behind the bushes. She was on a high."

"They like those highs, don't they?" Bob said, referring to our bipolar clients.

"Maybe you better get a bulletproof vest." A smile quirked at the corner of Mark's mouth. Probably from picturing me behind a bush.

"That's not funny," Debbie said.

"She's back on her meds, but she went into a depression today."

"At least you'll be safe for a while," Bob said.

I didn't want to talk about Mona's near miss anymore, or her condition. We chatted about their lives for a while before getting down to business.

After staffing, we dispersed to our offices.

My second client of the day was Karl Jankowski. I figured it would be a free hour, that I'd have time to catch up on paperwork. To my surprise he was sitting in the waiting room.

"Come on in," I said, feeling his eyes as I walked down the hall in front of him. "Have a seat." I motioned him to one of the two empty chairs, taking the desk chair myself. Rocking back, I appraised him. He'd cleaned up, but the telltale signs of a heavy drinker showed. Bloodshot eyes, wrinkles, broken blood vessels, rough, rosy skin.

He cleared his throat a couple of times and shifted his position. One foot bobbed up and down.

"How are you feeling?"

"Not good," he admitted.

"Want to talk about why?"

"I've got the mother of all hangovers, that's why," he said.

"Bad enough to consider going into a recovery program?"

Slouching lower in the chair, he tucked his hands in his armpits and began to shiver.

Although I couldn't smell it, I was pretty sure he'd been into the booze that morning. He looked like he needed to be in detox, like he was going into withdrawal. "When did they release you?"

"Early," he said, his teeth clicking as if he were cold.

"I think we better go to the hospital." *Delirium tremens*, I thought, always a risk with a heavy drinker. I should have left him at the hospital instead of sending him to jail to make a point.

"Why didn't you let me stay there yesterday?"

"Because you keep showing up in ER and never follow up with appointments. I can't help you if you don't try to change your behavior."

Feeling rather guilty, I took him to the hospital myself. He went voluntarily, still lucid but shaking violently.

III

Sally Schmidt met me for a late Wednesday lunch at Mary's Place, a small restaurant in an old building. Wood floors, brick walls, and high tin ceilings hung with fans gave it character. We'd agreed it was time we talked about Mona. I waved from my table as she strode my way.

She sat across from me and picked up the menu. "What are you having?"

"Soup and bread." I took a sip of water.

The waiter sashayed over, obviously gay and proud of it. "Are you ready to order, ladies, or do you want a few minutes?"

I looked at Sally. "Do you need a little time?"

She put down the menu. "Nope. I'll have the soup of the day with bread."

When he left, I said, "I've never had a chance to talk to you alone. I want to thank you for being so good to Mona."

Sally was pretty average looking until she smiled, which she did.

Briefly. It transformed her face. "Mona was a good friend to me in high school. I was the class nerd. She was popular. She took me under her wing."

I'd graduated the year before Mona entered high school, but when I'd come home the phone had rung mostly for her. She'd been a cheerleader. That should have told me something. Actually, I hadn't paid much attention to her then. Too self-involved.

"My partner wants to let her go. He says she's not pulling her weight." Her smile vanished, but her gaze still held mine.

My heart took the proverbial plunge. "Have you tried talking to her? You might have more influence. She's been off her meds. I told you that, didn't I?"

She drew a deep breath. "You and I know what that means, but my partner only knows that she can't seem to finish anything she starts. I fear for her."

So did I, but who said stuff like that? I looked at Sally with more interest. Her light brown hair turned under in a pageboy; her dark eyes concealed her thoughts; her clear skin looked like it seldom saw the light of day. She needed to get outside and taste the air, but didn't we all? It was early spring.

"Would you like to come to dinner?" I asked on impulse.

She looked startled, then stammered, "When?"

I shrugged. "How about this Saturday? Bring a friend." I didn't think she was married, but she might be in a relationship.

"I have no commitments for Saturday," she said.

I wanted to see her smile again, but I couldn't think of anything funny to say.

"I know you're a mental health worker for the county," she said.

"I'm in the crisis unit. We put out fires and counsel clients. I deal with many clients like my sister, people with bipolar disorder. I do better with them than with her."

She crushed crackers onto her soup. "You're siblings."

"Siblings are closer genetically than parents or children."

"Perhaps that's why we don't like it when our brothers or sisters tell us what to do."

18

I thought it strange that she seemed to be getting better looking by the minute. Perception is everything. "Right you are."

"What should I wear?" she asked.

"What? Oh, you mean Saturday. Jeans. We live in the country. I have to warn you, though. When Mona gets wind of your coming, she'll fix every course she can think of. Don't eat breakfast or lunch."

She rewarded me with a laugh, then choked on her water and gasped, "I believe it."

"She'll light every candle she can find and fill the place with flowers and talk you to death. That is, if she's out of this depression. If not, she'll bury herself under her covers in the dark."

She sobered, as I did. We both had experienced Mona's depressions.

She insisted on paying the bill, leaving a hefty tip, and we exited the building together. A cool wind tunneled down the avenue and we parted quickly. I walked back to the office, slightly elated and wondering why.

Saturday morning I began working on dinner. I'd shopped Friday after work, having phoned Sally to ask if there were any foods she or her friend avoided. None, she'd said, and she wasn't bringing a friend. I'd settled on carrot soup, pork tenderloin, steamed red potatoes and fresh green beans, and bread. For hors d'oeuvres, I'd fix roll-ups and a curry dip for raw veggies. I put a bottle of Ecco Domani pinot grigio in the fridge.

When Mona dragged herself downstairs around eleven in the morning, still in her pajamas, she asked who was coming to dinner.

"Your boss."

"Sally? You're serious?" She looked surprised.

"Yep."

She sat up straighter and showed some interest.

"You're better," I observed thankfully.

She was. She grated carrots for the soup and made brownies

from scratch. I'd forgotten about dessert. By late afternoon everything was prepared that could be done in advance.

Around five I stepped outside. A thin layer of clouds covered the sky. Warm southerly currents were blowing in. The ground had become a giant sponge. I stayed on the walk, sniffing at the hint of spring in the air.

Sally's BMW sedan purred up the muddy driveway. It looked as if she'd just run it through the car wash, and I cringed as dirt splattered the car.

Mona rushed out of the house and crowded against me, pushing me off the broken pavement. I wanted to tell her not to talk so much tonight, to listen instead, but she didn't take advice well.

Sally emerged from the sleek black car and tiptoed through the slop to the sidewalk. She wore white tennis shoes. What one needed out here were waterproof boots.

That was when I heard the sandhill cranes overhead, making their weird clacking sounds. Wings spread, long legs dangling, they swept down to land in the pasture beyond the empty barn. This was my first sighting of the year.

"Get the binoculars, will you, Mona?"

"Get them yourself," she snapped, forging past me toward Sally.

"She's my guest," I pointed out, sounding like a petulant child. I even plucked at Mona's sweater as if to hold her back, but she pulled loose.

"I remember being here," Sally said with one of those great smiles. She was becoming more attractive each time I saw her. "We worked on a float in your barn." The barn badly needed shoring up. It was about to implode, but the cost of restoring it was prohibitive.

"I want to do so much with this place," Mona said with an eye to the decrepit building.

"Look behind you, Sally," I interrupted.

She turned and shaded her eyes against the mild glare of the sun leaching through the clouds. "Sandhill cranes? They're back!" She clasped her hands together. I imagined her smile.

"I hope it means warmer weather." The earth gave off a slightly pungent odor, promising new growth.

Sally started back toward her car in slow motion, apparently thinking this would be less disturbing to the cranes. "I'll get my binoculars."

"See," I hissed at Mona.

"I'll get ours," she said. "Where are they?"

"In the whatnot drawer in the kitchen." I kept them handy. Over the winter we'd had evening and rose breasted grosbeaks along with the usual birds at the feeders.

We took turns standing by Sally's car, ignoring the mucky driveway and eyeing the sandhill cranes through binoculars. Mona had little patience for bird watching and quickly grew bored. She leaned against the BMW.

"I'd love to have one of these cars. What kind of mileage do you get?" she asked as if she could afford a BMW.

"Not very good. I've got a van for winter."

"Do you want to sell it? The BMW?" Mona said.

"There's nothing wrong with your Focus," I pointed out. I'd co-signed her car loan.

"It's boring. I want something exciting. What I'd really like is a sporty convertible, like this."

"Wouldn't we all," I said. I drove a Saturn wagon with ninety-six thousand miles on it.

"You are such a downer." Mona gave me an exasperated look. Her hair parted in the wind, showing white scalp and dark roots. Impatiently, she brushed it off her face. "You're against any change for the better." She snatched the binoculars off my nose. "Let me look."

I backed off, eyes watering. Confronting her when she was in a mood got us nowhere. She and Sally began comparing notes as the big birds took long strides across the field.

21

When the sandhill cranes took off, calling to each other, I suggested we go indoors. The sidewalk led to a small mud room, which opened to the kitchen and the garage. I hung my jacket on one of the hooks and took off my shoes.

Sally examined her tennis shoes. "I should take them off."

I handed her a pair of slipper socks. "You can wear these. We keep them for guests. Sorry about your shoes, though. I should have warned you," I said.

I'd pondered the question of liquor. Drinking exacerbated Mona's moods. Normally, I kept no alcohol in the house. While Sally and I stood in the kitchen, both of us uncertain as to what to say or do next, Mona took off through the dining room. I'd bought a bottle of vodka and hidden it in the back of a cupboard.

"Would you like a drink? The choices are limited—wine or vodka. I think I'll have a screwdriver."

"That'd be nice," she said.

I poured two drinks and handed Sally one, then took a big slug of mine. Immediately, I felt a buzz. Good. I needed to relax.

Before I'd gone outside, I'd set the hors d'oeuvres on the butcher block table in the middle of the kitchen.

"Help yourself. Then let's go where it's more comfortable."

Mona had set the dining room table. She'd dusted off the vase of silk flowers that always stood as a centerpiece, put tapered candles in crystal holders on either side of the flowers, and cleaned the flies out of the overhead light. The plates were our mother's hand-painted china. The silverware genuine. We'd have to wash everything by hand. We walked through to the living room.

Vintage Sixties with shag green carpet, blond Danish modern furniture, and worn lampshades. Maybe it was time to redecorate. Candles smoked on the mantelpiece and all the tables, lending the room an air of intimacy. I turned on every lamp. "Looks like we're having a séance," I joked, embarrassed that she might think I was trying at romance.

"Well, you said there would be candles," Sally reminded me with a laugh.

We sat at opposite ends of the couch. I studied a cobweb attached to and floating above the floor lamp on her end of the sofa. Another uncomfortable silence settled over us, so that I was glad when Mona came into the room.

"Starting without me?" she asked accusingly.

"I didn't know where you were," I said. "Go fix yourself a plate."

She returned quickly with all the hors d'oeuvres, which she arranged on the coffee table. "What are you drinking?" she asked.

"There's pop in the fridge." She already knew that.

"I want a real drink. Is it vodka?"

"I'll fix you one."

"Oh no, you don't. You won't put anything in it," she said, narrowing her eyes.

"Yes, I will." I'd put a few drops of vodka in it. "You entertain Sally." I took my glass with me, knowing she was not above drinking from it.

Her strident voice carried into the kitchen, two rooms away. I caught Don Janssen's name, the other partner in the law firm. Hurrying with the drink, I carried it to the living room.

Sitting down, I popped a roll-up in my mouth, then chomped nervously on a carrot. I never should have gotten the bottle of wine. Mona would demand some of that too. Sally might just fire her after this evening.

"He doesn't like me," Mona was saying. "He wants to get rid of me, doesn't he?"

"Sally didn't come here to talk work," I interjected.

"No, that's okay." Sally waved a hand at me. "He doesn't dislike you, Mona. It's not personal."

"He thinks I'm not doing my job?" Mona's voice rose and hovered between us.

Sally leaned forward and put her drink down. "I know you can do the job."

"*You* think I'm not doing my job?" Mona wasn't dumb. Her tone dropped to a lower level.

Sally took a deep breath. "I think you can do a better job than you have been the past few weeks. I know you can."

Mona exploded. "I work hard."

"I know you do," Sally soothed.

Somehow we got through the evening. I silently vowed never to invite anyone over again. When I walked Sally out to her car, Mona followed us, so there was no way to apologize.

"See you at work, Mona," Sally said, and to me, "Thanks for the great dinner."

"Thanks for coming." I managed a smile.

She turned the BMW around. Mona and I watched as the night swallowed the taillights.

"Think she had a good time?" Mona asked.

"Almost as good I did," I said.

IV

Sunday morning I woke to the cooing of mourning doves. Sunlight filtering through the film on the windows shafted across the floor and climbed onto my quilt, warming me. I felt almost happy. I'd been dreaming that Sally and I were stalking a couple of sandhill cranes through tall grass. The flapping of cranes' wings had turned into doves taking flight.

Then I recalled the previous evening and slid under the covers with a moan. If I'd known Sally's home number, I'd have called her from the bedside phone. Perhaps, though, it was better to let a little time pass. What would I say? What could I say? I was tired of making excuses for Mona.

Downstairs, sunshine flowed through the windows, showing how badly they needed a wash. Mona was in the kitchen preparing a huge breakfast. "You treated me last night. Now I'm going to treat you," she said.

The phone rang and I picked the receiver off the wall where it had hung since I was a kid. "Hello. Abby here."

"Hi, your dad here." I heard a smile in his voice. He and Mom were happy in Arizona. Craig, my brother, lived nearby. Craig had a spouse and three kids. Mona and I had none. "How are you two?"

"All right." Dad didn't want the boat rocked. I think he and Mom had left Mona in my hands because they'd had enough of her aberrant behavior. Being a psychiatric social worker qualified me in their view. "What's new with you?"

"Your mom's golf game hit a new low."

"Is that good?" I asked, turning my back to Mona who was gesturing she wanted to talk.

"In golf it is. She won a new set of clubs."

"Good for her. It's a gorgeous day here. When are you and Mom coming for a visit?"

"When are you? It's time you made the trip."

"We're so busy at work right now, I don't know how I could get away."

My mother came on the line. I missed them both, but I missed her more. It had been a year since I'd seen either one.

"Hi, honey," Mom said. "How are you?"

"Okay." I knew she'd pick up on the highs and lows in my tones.

"Honest?" she asked, and went on without an answer. "Why don't you and Mona fly down here? We'll pay the airfare."

"That's nice, Mom. I'd love to, but work is so busy."

"It's always busy, Abby. Give us some dates and we'll get the tickets."

I was sorely tempted. March is a good time to escape Wisconsin, but the month was nearly over.

Mona snatched the phone from me, banging my ear. "I'll come."

I wrestled the phone back in a fit of pique. "Mom? Can you still hear?"

"Mona could live with us, you know."

26

"She could live on her own," I muttered, stepping into the mud room and closing the door.

"I'm sorry, honey. I know she isn't easy." What they'd found hardest to swallow had been Mona's large appetite for sex, which wasn't unusual for someone with bipolar disorder.

"She's settled down a lot." She hadn't picked up anyone in months.

"But it doesn't give you much of a life of your own."

"I'm too busy anyway." I wanted to see Mom. "Why don't you and Dad come here?" Mona and I could alternate days off.

"If you can't come, send Mona. It'll give you a break."

I turned the phone over to Mona. Mom had got it right. I wanted to see them, but not with Mona. That would be too much like work.

Sally left a message on my voice mail during Monday's staff meeting, thanking me for the dinner. I phoned and left a message on hers, saying I was glad she came over, that maybe we could do lunch again.

Karl Jankowski was out of the hospital and slotted for nine o'clock. Instead, I ushered into my office an elderly couple, mid-seventies, who shouted at each other the entire time. They were walk-ins, the wife insisting they were in crisis, that she was on the verge of doing harm to herself or him. If Karl hadn't been a no-show, I would never have seen them.

"She's cheating on me," the husband yelled in the first few minutes.

"Who'd want to have sex with you, you old goat," his wife shouted back.

"See, what'd I tell you?" He jabbed his finger at the woman. "She won't do her wifely duty."

"Oh, duty tooty to you," the wife retorted.

I wondered who'd want to have sex with either one of them. I knew people made love at every age, but these two had no obvious appeal, certainly not to each other. Sex is a mind game.

When I was able to get a word in, I suggested they begin with a dialogue, ladies first.

The wife told how he followed her around while she washed clothes, made beds, cooked and cleaned, grocery shopped, insisting that she drop everything and have sex with him.

He interrupted periodically. "Not true, not true."

I turned to him. "What is true?"

"She could stop doing those things. It don't take long to have a quickie."

I swallowed a smile. "What if you set aside a certain time every day for some intimacy?"

"That mean sex?" he asked suspiciously.

"Morning might be a good time. After breakfast, while the sun's shining."

"He'll forget as soon as it's done. More likely, he won't be able to do it." She snorted.

"Is that a problem?" I asked him.

"Is what a problem?" He glared at his wife.

"Limp as a noodle," his wife said. "It's got no spring." She chortled.

"Why don't you just hold each other and talk a little? Maybe something will happen," I said, now fighting a grin.

"Fat chance," she said.

"She's always too tired," he complained.

"If you helped once in a while, maybe I wouldn't be," she shot back.

"You know, your wife will respond to you better if you do help her." I glanced at my watch.

The woman struggled to her feet on thick legs and grabbed her husband by the arm. "Come on, you worthless old man. I told you this was a waste of time." She looked at me as her husband pushed himself out of the chair. "No offense, miss. There's nothing to work with here, is all. He's mostly gone." She tapped her head.

28

I stood up, too. "Why don't you make an appointment with one of the family counselors on your way out?"

"Nothing's gonna help him."

They shuffled arm in arm down the hall.

My co-workers from crisis, whose offices were adjacent or across the hall from mine, stuck their heads out of their doors and grinned.

I was saved from their commentary by the ringing phone. Shutting my door, I picked up.

"Hi, it's me, Sally. Want to have lunch on Friday?"

"Sure. How's Mona doing?" I asked warily, fearing she wanted to tell me in person that she was firing Mona.

"She's putting out three times the work anyone else is. Don's impressed."

It was hard to know what was normal behavior for Mona. I suspected she was on her way back to a manic state. "Want to meet at Mary's again?"

"My treat."

"You treated last time."

"You fed me dinner Saturday night."

"Okay." I wanted to see her, I realized, if only to explain Saturday night.

This time she got to the restaurant before I did. She was sitting at the same table. The same waiter was putting coffee down in front of her as I walked up.

"A cup of decaf for me, please," I said.

"Okey-dokey." He turned my cup over and poured.

"Thanks." I looked at the menu and ordered the soup of the day and bread.

"Same here," she said.

"You ladies are easy to please." He strutted off to place the order.

I looked into Sally's plain face, which I no longer found so ordinary. Her steady dark gaze looked wise, her brown hair hung thick around a slender neck. Rather than pale, her skin appeared unblemished, like porcelain. I was waiting for the smile to turn it all on. "You said Mona was doing well at work?"

"She's caught up on everything she'd neglected."

I noticed Sally tearing her napkin to bits and thought I should be the one shredding napkins and placemats. It was Mona who had embarrassed me in front of Sally at my house.

"I want to apologize for Saturday night," I began, burning my mouth on the coffee. "Damn, that's hot."

"You okay?"

"Yeah." I set the cup down.

"I had a fine time Saturday night," she said.

"I wanted to tape Mona's mouth shut."

She rewarded me with a laugh. "She always talks a lot, unless she's depressed. She sure bounced out of that in a hurry."

"Thankfully. I've seen her so depressed I was afraid to leave her alone for more than a few minutes." It struck me that Mona was dominating the conversation without even being there. She would have loved that.

Sally gave me a smile. "I'm used to Mona."

"She must have been awfully good to you in high school."

"She was. I won't let Don fire her."

I found myself staring at her smile. "That's so good of you."

"I'm not being good, believe me. Now tell me more about yourself. How do you happen to be living with Mona?"

I told her how our parents had asked me to move in with Mona before they left for Arizona. Rent free. How could I turn it down? "But it's like being at work twenty-four hours a day."

The waiter put the soup and bread on the table and left. She crumbled her crackers in their cellophane. "Sometimes you sleep, don't you? Sometimes Mona sleeps, doesn't she?"

"I sleep more. She's awake half the night, sometimes all of it." Here we were again, talking about Mona.

"How did you happen to become a social worker?" she asked.

"I thought it might be rewarding. It is most of the time." There were the Karl Jankowskis who sometimes used the system, but there were also the Anna Pagents who really needed us.

I asked, "How about you? Why did you become an attorney?"

"I love the law," she said. "I find it exciting, and often we do help people."

"Memorizing all those cases, looking for precedents, defending the guilty?"

"The majority of our work is estates, businesses, divorces. We never chase ambulances."

"I didn't think you did."

"Do you like living in the country?"

"I think I'd rather be in town." When I got home at night, it was hard to make myself drive back for an evening out. If I lived in the city, I'd go to concerts, movies, plays, the library. At least, I thought I would.

When we parted, she asked if we could have lunch again next week.

"Same place, same time, unless I hear from you. How does that sound?"

"Good."

We were on the sidewalk in the cool breeze. The spring we'd caught a glimpse of over the weekend was gone. I started walking toward the office.

V

I pushed the doorbell, then let myself in with the key Nance had given me a few years ago when she and Dennis had bought the house. I stayed at their home when on call, because the drive from home to town was six miles. Setting my bag on the floor of the foyer, I went looking for my old friend.

I nearly bumped into her as she came out of a bedroom, a dust rag draped over her shoulder. "Is this the weekend on call?" she asked as if I hadn't reminded her earlier in the week.

"You forgot?"

She ushered me toward the kitchen. "There was a message on the voice mail for Dennis from someone named Shirley."

"Shirley who?" I sat at the kitchen table in the windowed nook. The light shining in gave the illusion of spring. She poured me a cup of coffee and herself a glass of wine.

"Dennis has gone to a conference in Madison without me. Of course, I didn't really want to go."

"I never miss a chance to go to Madison," I said, trying to keep the disappointment out of my voice. I liked Dennis. He was more fun than Nance. It was disloyal, but it was true.

A worried look crossed her face. "Our sex life has really tapered off."

"That does happen after a few years, I hear." Was she suggesting Dennis was having an affair?

She refocused. "By the way, that makes me wonder about your sex life."

I studied her for a moment, then sighed. "I don't want to even think about it."

"Anybody on the horizon?"

"Nope."

She placed her hand with its long tapered fingers on my forearm. "Honey, you need to get your ass in gear. You're one cute chick."

"Apparently cute isn't enough, but that's kind of you." I was uncomfortable with compliments, never quite sure how to reply.

"I'm not being kind, sweetie. You're a knockout." She slugged back her wine, and the phone rang. "Hello. Nance speaking. Yes, she is. Hang on." Handing me the receiver, she poured herself more wine.

I'd given Nance's number to the phone workers. Sarah said, "Remember James Brume? Turn on channel five. He held his ex-girlfriend at gunpoint on Nile Street earlier today. He's in jail, charged with shooting her."

Brume was one of those guys who thought he owned a woman. His ex-girlfriend, Elizabeth Halbertson, had obtained a restraining order against him, but that hadn't stopped him from harassing her. I remembered him as a scrawny, cocky guy with a narrow face and close-set eyes. I'd met her, too. A frightened, overweight young woman.

"Okay if I turn on the news?" I said to Nance.

"Go ahead."

A young news anchor, hunched into his windbreaker, nose red and hair blowing, was standing outside a gray frame house, talking to the camera. "Earlier today James Brume held a woman hostage here in the house behind me. He shot her just before the police stormed the building. He's under arrest, and the woman remains in stable condition in the hospital."

I slid into a leather chair and leaned forward.

"Jesus Christ," Nance breathed, "where is he when you need him. God, I hope she's going to be okay. Don't you just hate those fuckers who think they own a woman?"

"Yes." I had no sympathy for abusers or child molesters. No matter that they'd probably been abused and molested themselves.

We ordered a pizza and ate it in front of the TV while we watched a movie. I was on edge, waiting for the phone to ring. Men like Brume often threaten suicide when they're imprisoned. They can't stand it when their victims escape their influence. He'd probably rather have Halbertson dead than alive and out from under his thumb.

When I went to bed in the guest room, I snuggled under the covers and listened to the wind blowing outside. It felt more like the middle of winter instead of the end of March.

Not once all day had I thought of Mona. I should have called her after work, but the evening's events drove everything else out of my mind.

I drifted into the nonsense of a dream and woke at the first ring, fumbling for the receiver. It was three in the morning, and the phone rang in Nance's room, too. "Abby Dean here."

"Abby." It was Mona. I sat up and propped pillows behind me. "Do you know what time it is?"

"I was painting the living room. I didn't look at the clock."

"Go to bed, Mona. It's always better to paint when it's light outside."

"I know. Why didn't you phone?"

"I was out on call, and then it was too late." Actually, it was never too late. Mona slept so little. "I'm sorry." I was, knowing she must be lonely.

"When are you coming home?"

"Monday after work. I'm on call till Monday morning. Remember? Will you be okay?"

"I guess I'll have to be."

"Wait for me. I'll help with the painting." We had picked out colors the weekend before. "You'll probably have to use two or three coats on the front hall." On the walls she had covered with blood red latex.

She talked on awhile. I fell back on the pillows and began to drift off. Finally I said, "I have to keep the line open in case work calls. I'll talk to you tomorrow, Mona. Get some sleep."

I woke again when Nance knocked once before entering the room. "Coffee call."

I looked at the clock. It was nine. Throwing my legs over the edge of the bed, I sat up. "I never sleep this late."

Even this early in the morning, Nance looked terrific. Her blonde hair shone in the light. She was dressed in an elegant robe, fastened over pale green silky pajamas. The trouble with great-looking friends is that one suffers in comparison. She put my coffee on the bedside table and sat beside me with her own cup. She smelled like baby powder.

"Did you have to go out last night? I heard the phone ring."

"It was Mona. She was painting the walls at three in the morning."

"Doesn't she ever sleep?"

"That's the manic part of being bipolar."

"Oh, to have all that energy." She sipped the brew.

I snorted into my coffee. "You don't want it, believe me. She can't stop pacing and talking. She can't sleep. It's a curse."

"Should we go see what she's done?"

"We'll have to take two vehicles or you'll have to go along with me if I get called."

"What are your plans for today?"

"I thought I'd go into the office and catch up on a few things."

"Forget work. I've got better things in mind for us. Come on down and eat."

"Let me shower first."

"Hurry. I only serve breakfast till ten-thirty. Same as McDonald's." She swished out the door, managing to look sexy. If we hadn't been friends forever, I might have been attracted to her.

In the afternoon we went to an open house at a new antique mall. We cruised through booths filled with musty furniture, old lamps, ticking clocks, Victrolas, dolls and toys from long ago, books with loose pages, boxes of postcards written by people long dead to people also deceased, pictures in old frames, hand tools from another time, wooden bowls, magazines from earlier generations. All the detritus from other lives sold as antiques and collectibles. It was kind of sad when thought about that way.

The dealers bought the stuff at estate and garage sales, from other dealers, even at Goodwill Industries. I lived with the furniture from my youth, already considered collectible by some. I preferred new.

Nance plucked a glass of wine off a tray and stopped to talk, while I moved on, weaving my way through the furniture, the copper vats, the crocks. We had a couple of crocks at home which we filled with potatoes and onions.

Picking up a book, I turned the pages. It was a paperback by Lisa Alther, *Other Women*, which I'd read years ago. Neither an antique nor a collectible. I tucked it under my arm and looked around for a piece of furniture to sit on. Most of the seats on the chairs and sofas were roped off.

Finding a straight-backed chair near the front door, I immersed myself in the book. Halfway through the first chapter, the cell phone went off, startling me. I fished it out of my pocket. "Abby Dean."

"I thought you were going to call," Mona said accusingly.

"Have you been asleep yet?"

"I'm not done with the painting yet."

"Are you taking your meds?"

36

"Quit asking me that. That and whether I've been to sleep. I'm only four years younger than you. What are you doing?"

"I'm on call. Remember?"

"I know that." I heard the radio in the background and maybe the TV.

"I'll come out, but I can't stay."

"You don't have to."

Dropping Nancy's Audi off at the hospital in case I got called, we drove past brown fields under a gray sky. Dried, broken corn stalks shuddered in the cold wind. I walked into the house with Nance on my heels, and stopped dead at the door to the dining room. The place looked like a modern painting. Bold strokes, angling in all directions, covered the walls and woodwork. The carpet was splotched with the fallout.

Breakfast burned up my throat and I swallowed it back down. "Goddamn it all to hell," I said, fighting back the urge to find Mona and beat her to death.

Nance stood just inside the dining room, her mouth agape. "What a fucking mess."

"Mona," I yelled, going into the living room which was in the same sorry state. Paint on the green shag, the woodwork. She'd had enough sense to cover the furniture with sheets, but they were good sheets, ones we used on our beds.

Nance pulled up behind me and tapped me on the shoulder. "Dennis can clean this up. He's good at restoration." She looked alarmed. I wasn't sure if she was afraid of what I might do to Mona or of Mona herself.

I sat down, fighting back tears. It would be easier to burn the place down than to try to get the paint off everything. I didn't want to go upstairs and see any more and was almost relieved when work called. A teenager had overdosed on Tylenol and was at the hospital, having her stomach pumped. I'd have to go.

Mona came down the stairs, carrying a can of paint. She resembled a statue splattered with pigeon droppings. Paint in her hair, on her skin, her clothes. Had she done this on purpose? She hadn't smeared paint where it didn't belong when she'd created the naked ladies on my bedroom wall nor when she'd turned the front hallway blood red.

I felt a murderous anger. Jerking the paint can away from her, I strode through the house till I found the others and carried them outside to my car. "No more painting. You hear?"

I didn't hang around to listen to her response. I had to get away before I inflicted serious damage on her.

VI

My cell phone rang as I left the hospital. Nance had gone home when we reached the hospital.

"James Brume is on a rampage, threatening suicide, yelling, getting everyone in an uproar. They want someone to talk to him, to calm him down."

Although I knew it was a waste of time, that I'd probably make him angrier, I'd have to try.

I checked in at the desk at the jail. "I'm Abby Dean from crisis, here to see James Brume."

"I'll page someone to take you in." The woman in uniform smiled at me. "I know you, don't I?"

I read her nametag without making a connection and smiled in return. "I'm sure you do."

"I should warn you, he's madder than hell. When they usually threaten to kill themselves, they're kind of quiet. Not this guy. He'd tear the place down if he could."

"So I was told." I always thought it strange how the ones who should be the most apologetic were usually the angriest. They saw themselves as victims, claiming someone or something else drove them to do whatever they did. "Surprise, surprise," I added. He wasn't suicidal. More like it, he was murderous.

The officer on duty, Scott McLane, took me to the cell. I'd seen him here on other trips and at ER. "I remember you."

"I remember you, too. Sorry you had to come."

I shrugged. "It's part of the job." A disagreeable one and usually a waste of time.

Brume's profanity grew louder as we approached his cell. When he saw me, he spat, "Bitch."

Despite the bars between us, I nearly stepped backward. I much preferred Anna Pagent calling me a bitch. A helpless anger and misguided sense of self-preservation drove her, but she was a paper tiger. Brume's anger was aimed at anyone who came between him and his possessions. Had we stolen his car he would not feel less wronged.

His hands gripped the metal. "You turned my girlfriend against me."

"Why do you think that?" I kept my voice calm, unemotional. It would be unprofessional to react to his anger.

"You people shot her, not me," he screamed. "If you'd left us alone, she'd be okay."

Scott's jaw muscles tensed, his skin flushed. He took a few steps till he stood next to me. I appreciated his gesture of support, felt strengthened by it, but maintained eye contact with Brume.

"You said something about killing yourself. Do you want to tell me about it?" I kept talking although I knew it was a waste of time. I'd been taught not to show fear in situations like this, but that didn't stop me from feeling it. I might become a target of Brume's anger should he get out on bail.

"With you? You told her to get that restraining order." He shook the unshakable bars. "I want to talk to someone else."

I left after ten unproductive minutes.

"Sorry about that," Scott said, escorting me out of the cellblock as Brume yelled obscenities at our backs.

"It's not your fault. You had to call me in."

Outside, I shuddered as I welcomed the cool wind, hoping it would blow the threat of Brume away.

Driving to Nance's, I attempted to clear my mind, but Mona kept creeping in. I wished she were flying out to visit Mom and Dad on Monday, that I wouldn't have to face her for at least a week.

I'd cooled down enough to think about what I was going to do about the paint job gone awry. Dennis would point me in the right direction. I didn't expect him to do the work. At least, he'd know how to remove the paint from the woodwork. Dennis built houses for a nonprofit group called A Home Of Your Own.

Dennis's truck sat in the driveway. I parked in front of the third garage door, the one where they kept the boat. I sure was in the wrong profession. Of course, they both worked. Low interest rates had spurred the real estate market and Nance to new selling heights.

"Hey, woman." Dennis hugged me when I went into the kitchen. I melted into his muscular frame. There's something about a confident man that makes me yearn to be straight. Only momentarily, though. He wore jeans and a baggy sweatshirt and smelled like the outdoors. "I thought you were Nance."

"Where is she?"

"Showing a house. She left a note." He lifted a piece of paper and dropped it on the table.

"Did you skip out on your conference?" I asked.

"It ended at noon. Why didn't someone tell me you'd be here?"

"Nance must have forgotten."

He rolled his eyes. "How's Mona?"

I told him what she'd done to the house. "There's paint on the woodwork, the floors."

"Want me to take a look at it?"

"Would you? I'd be so grateful for some advice."

41

"Let's go." He picked up his keys.

"We'll have to drive separate vehicles. I'm on call."

"That's okay, isn't it?"

I sighed at the thought of seeing Mona, but I felt I should go at his convenience. "Sure."

We turned into my driveway and parked in front of the garage. Unlocking the kitchen door, we stepped inside. When we reached the dining room, Dennis, who was looking over my shoulder, breathed in sharply.

"Mona," I yelled, the anger rising again.

No answer.

I went through the house, calling her name, checking the rooms, and felt relief when I couldn't find her. I needed time away to get over my anger. I'd look in the garage before leaving to see if her car was gone.

Downstairs, Dennis was standing in the center of the living room. "How far did she get upstairs?" He looked around. "Actually it's kind of creative. Sort of like an abstract painting."

I thought of the naked ladies in my bedroom, still intact, and was surprised at how much that meant to me. "She didn't get that far."

"I'll send someone out to clean up the woodwork."

"I don't expect you to." Or did I? A spurt of hope took hold. It gave me energy.

He waved a hand. "This would take you forever." He smiled. "She did a number, didn't she? Where is she anyway?"

"I don't know," I said, hoping she wasn't out buying more paint. "Listen, I'll pay for the labor and materials."

"We'll talk about that later. Let me see what can be done first." He looked at the floor. "What do you want to do about the carpets?"

"Throw them away." They were dusty and dark and out of date.

"Good idea," he agreed. "What's underneath them? Do you know?"

"Probably plywood."

"You pick out some carpeting. We'll pull out the old and put in the new. I'll send Shirley. She does good work."

"Nance said there was a message for you from Shirley," I said.

"Would you believe Shirley's a man, wanting to be a woman?" He grinned.

"Serious?"

"Yep. She's my best worker, but she hates wearing jeans."

I laughed.

On the way out, I checked the garage. Mona's Focus was gone. I wasn't so angry now that Dennis had offered to send help. Maybe this was the push I needed to make some changes in the house.

When we got back to Nance and Dennis's house, Nance's car was parked inside the open garage. Dennis drove into the other bay, came outside, and closed both doors.

He unlocked the front door. "Hello, it's only us," he said, stepping aside for me to go first.

"In the kitchen," Nance called.

"Did Nance see your place?" Dennis asked.

"She was with me when I went out there," I said, wondering what Mona was up to.

"Where've you two been?" Nance asked.

"Looking at Mona's paint job," Dennis said.

"I told you he'd take care of it." Nance gave me a pleased smile.

"I can't let him do it gratis," I interjected.

Dennis put his arm around my shoulders and gave me a hug. "We'll talk money later."

"How was the conference?" Nance asked, looking at him intently.

"Pretty good. Talked to a lot of contractors doing the sort of thing we're doing. Lots of good people." He moved to put his arm around her shoulders. "Any messages?"

"Shirley called."

"What did Shirley have to say?" he asked, lifting his eyebrows.

"That she was sick and was taking Saturday off. She didn't go to the conference?"

"She isn't a member of the confederation. She's my best worker."

Nance trained a disbelieving gaze on her husband. "I didn't know you had a woman on the job."

"Not yet, but soon. Technically, Shirley's still a man. When she gets enough money together, she's gonna take care of that."

Nance looked puzzled. "Shirley who? Have I met her? Him?"

"Shawn. I don't know why she chose Shirley when she could have been Shawna, but she did." He got down a couple of glasses. "Want a drink, Nance? I know you can't have one, Abby."

"Shawn wants to be Shirley? Why would he do that? He's so good looking."

"Shirley's a looker, too. When she turns into a woman, she'll be a hot commodity," Dennis said, fighting a grin and losing.

"You've got your own hot commodity," Nance shot back.

I laughed at the ridiculous conversation, and Dennis hugged Nance.

"You owe me an apology, you know," he said.

"Why? I didn't accuse you of anything," Nance retorted.

"Not in so many words. You were thinking it."

As we finished dinner, my cell phone went off. "Abby Dean speaking."

"Are you still mad at me?"

"Why'd you do it, Mona?" I asked, relieved that she'd called.

"It was night and kind of dark. I see now what a mess I made."

"It's going to be a costly mess," I said, carrying my plate to the dishwasher.

"I'll pay." There was a pause in which we breathed at each other. "You're not coming home till Monday night?"

"No. Why?"

"Just double checking."

"Look, Mona. Don't do anything to the house without talking to me first."

"I won't. Got to go now." She hung up.

The three of us cleaned up the kitchen and went into the other room to watch a movie. Dennis fell asleep in the middle of it. It was more of a chick flick, and Nance and I watched it to the end.

"Hope you get to sleep through the night," she said as we went to bed.

It was no big deal if I was called out on Saturday night. I could sleep in on Sunday. But if I was up part of Sunday night or all of it, I'd still have to go to work on Monday. Those were the rules. If you were on call, you made it to work the next day for staffing.

I got through Saturday night undisturbed and handled Sunday's incidents over the phone. I could hardly believe my luck when I awoke Monday morning at six-thirty, never having to leave the bed during the night. After showering and eating a couple of pieces of toast, I thanked Dennis and Nance, and headed out the door.

VII

After work, I collected Mona's airline tickets from the travel agent. Still no warm weather. Only the prospect of ten days without Mona kept me from turning around and getting a ticket to Arizona myself.

I pulled up next to a panel truck parked in front of the garage. The lettering on the side read Longworth Construction and Remodeling Inc., Dennis's company.

Carrying my briefcase inside, I set it down in the kitchen. A laughing Mona talked animatedly from the dining room. Whoever replied wasn't Dennis. I walked toward their voices.

Someone close to six feet tall, with slim hips and long legs stood next to Mona. They turned toward me, and I realized this person must be Shirley. She had wonderful high cheekbones, greenish blue eyes, full lips, a square chin, a pronounced Adam's apple, and a hint of breasts hidden beneath a flannel shirt. Wavy blond hair hung to her chin.

I moved forward to shake her hand. "I'm Abby Dean, Mona's sister."

Shirley showed off dimples and straight teeth. "You're Dennis's friend. I'm Shirley Young."

"She's going to take care of this mess, aren't you?" Mona said.

"I'm gonna try," Shirley promised.

"You can get the paint off the woodwork?" I asked.

"I think so."

"Vandals," Mona put in. "They should be strung up."

I looked at Mona with surprise. "Yes. By their toes." I was sure Dennis had told Shirley the story, certain I saw it in her eyes.

"I wish I was as tall as you are," Mona said irrelevantly. "The better to reach the top shelves."

"It's an advantage in this business. I brought some paint remover to try out on the woodwork."

"Are you hungry?" Mona asked. "I was just going to fix dinner." Batting her eyelashes, she motioned toward the kitchen. If I hadn't known better, I would have thought she was flirting. Maybe she was confused. Mona had always been straight, but even I was having trouble thinking of Shirley as a she. Probably because I knew technically she was still a he.

"I brought a sandwich."

"You can eat it with us," Mona persisted.

"I better get started on this," Shirley said, going out to the van.

"What's for supper?" I asked, once she was gone.

"I find her so attractive. Do you think I'm like you?"

"No," I said. "You were going to fix dinner?"

Mona's tone became all business. "Tuna fish salad sandwiches. I'm busy packing. Did you pick up my tickets?"

"Yes." I handed them to her and went to change clothes.

When I came downstairs, Shirley was brushing a thick liquid onto the painted woodwork. "If Mona and I help, won't this go faster?"

"First let's see if it's going to work."

I found Mona in the kitchen, heating up a can of tomato soup

47

to go with the sandwiches. "We're going to have to help, you know."

"I don't mind," she said.

Friday morning when I took Mona to the airport, Shirley hadn't yet finished with the dining room. My knees were sore from crawling along the floor, scraping off the paint. I'd told her I'd work at it over the weekend, but she said she was coming back on Saturday.

Clouds hung low overhead, thick with unfallen snow, although it was the first weekend of April. Mona was getting out of the paint removal and the shitty weather. Life was never fair. People didn't get their just desserts. Then I reminded myself that Mona hadn't gotten a fair deal herself. She was the one who was bipolar, not me.

I drove to the airport doors and helped her move her luggage to the United Airlines counter. After giving her a hug and telling her to give my love to everyone, I continued on to work.

It occurred to me as I drove away that maybe Mona would like Arizona so much she'd stay there. I wasn't sure I wanted that either, though, as I thought about how lonely the house would be without her. I just needed a little break.

In the afternoon snow started to fall. It swirled around the parking lot, covering the vehicles with a thin white veneer. I'd invited Sally Shields to dinner Friday night and wondered if she'd cancel. When the phone rang around four, I figured it was her.

Instead, Nance said, "We're getting snowed in here. Mona's gone, right? Want to stay at our house tonight?"

I would have done so had it not been for Sally. "Can't. My company hasn't canceled. I will if that happens."

We chatted a few more minutes, then hung up. It didn't matter if we got eight inches, weather wasn't recognized as an excuse for not going to work or leaving early, not when you worked for the county. You could take a vacation day or a sick day but not a snow day.

I slid home on the country roads. The falling snow fell in behind the plow in front of me, covering the cleared pavement within minutes. The good thing about an April snowfall, though, is that it doesn't stick around long. The neighboring farmer plowed us out when necessary. We'd had almost no snow when we could have enjoyed it, so this seemed like an unkind joke. Everyone was focused on spring.

I found Dennis's panel truck parked outside the garage as it had been all week. That meant Shirley was hard at work inside, while Mona had escaped into the sunshine. Right now she was probably basking in its rays on my parents' porch. I welcomed the peace awaiting me.

Tracking snow into the mud room, I took off my shoes and followed the sound of the radio. Shirley looked down at me from the ladder where she was scraping paint off the ceiling trim.

"It's snowing like crazy out there," I said.

"An April fool's joke."

I admired the progress she'd made over the week, coming over after working on Dennis's other jobs. The woodwork was emerging once again, lighter. It must have darkened from years of neglect.

"I thought I'd work late tonight. I might not be able to make it back on Saturday."

"If you stay much longer, you won't get out of the driveway." I wondered if Sally would mind Shirley's presence. "You can eat with us."

"I thought Mona left for Arizona."

"She did, early this morning. A friend's coming over, if she can get here."

"I don't want to interrupt anything."

"It's no big deal. Join us. Hey, I can't thank you enough for all your work." I gestured at the walls, which looked less like the work of a mad artist and more like intended decor.

Upstairs, I changed into jeans and a sweatshirt, smiled a hello at the naked ladies, and clambered down to the kitchen. I'd made a balsamic marinade for the salmon yesterday and now I brushed it over the fillets. Nuking several potatoes, I chopped up red and yellow and green peppers. When the potatoes were done, I'd scoop out the insides, mash them, put them back in the potato skins with the peppers, then pop them back in the microwave. Next I made a salad. None of this took very long.

I went back into the dining room where Shirley was finishing

49

up. "Done for now," she said emphatically. She covered the can of paint remover and climbed off the ladder. Walking into the living room with her hands pressed into the small of her back, she looked around. "I think this is not so bad. It looks like the vandals were running out of steam. Don't you think?"

Did she really not know Mona was responsible for the damage? "Definitely."

"Your insurance should pay for everything." She turned and smiled at me. I hadn't thought about my insurance forking over any money. If I was to ask them to do that, I should have called them right away and never told anyone the truth. I figured it was too late for them to bail me out now.

The doorbell rang and I hurried to the kitchen. Sally stood on the stoop, ankle deep in snow. I flung open the door, and she stepped into the mud room.

"You actually made it," I said with pleased surprise.

"I see I'm not the only one who made it."

"Shirley works for a friend of mine. She's cleaning up the woodwork and tearing up carpet." I hadn't said anything about Mona's paint job. I was afraid Sally might think Mona was dangerously unpredictable, that she might destroy records or something. Perhaps I was doing them both a disservice.

Sally said, "The wind's picking up." It rattled the door behind her. The house had serious leaks, letting out the warmth, replacing it with cold.

Shirley was filling the dining room doorway when we entered the brightly lit kitchen. I introduced Sally, whose small hand disappeared into Shirley's. Next to Sally, Shirley looked like an amazon, but if Shirley's appearance surprised Sally, it didn't show.

"Are you staying for dinner?" I asked. "You're more than welcome."

"I better not," Shirley said, her voice a pleasant contralto. "I'll never get out of here."

"Oh well, we have plenty of beds. Have a drink with us anyway before you go." I'd bought some bloody Mary mix and tonic to go with the vodka and gave them my limited choices. "There's also wine—red and white."

"Vodka and tonic sounds good." Shirley sat in the chair I'd pulled out for her.

"I'll have a bloody Mary," Sally said, sitting across the table, leaving the seat between them for me. "Please."

I put some cheese and crackers on the table. We sat in silence for a moment or two, munching and drinking, while I considered what to say. The wind nagged at the window panes and siding.

"How long have you worked for Dennis?" I asked.

"A couple of years." Shirley took a gulp, draining a third of the glass.

"The same Dennis Longworth who builds houses for A Home Of Your Own?" Sally inquired.

Shirley nodded. I was impressed. "Do you know Dennis? His wife, Nance, is my oldest friend."

"I know him. He sometimes requests zoning changes. I'm on the board."

"The zoning board?"

She nodded and smiled wryly. "Which means long, boring meetings on Thursday nights once a month."

"Well, you must think it's important," I said. Why else bother?

"What we need is a zoning plan for this area, instead of run-away growth."

Shirley had now finished her drink. She stood up. "I better get going. Thanks for the drink."

"Thanks for all the help."

"I'll be back Monday for sure."

A gust of cold, snowy air rushed in as she went out the door. I turned on the outside light and peered at the swirling flakes. It seriously looked like winter outside.

I asked Sally if she wanted another drink. She said she'd have a glass of wine, if I wanted to open a bottle. Determined to make the most of my ten days of freedom, I refilled my drink—although already I felt the effects of the alcohol.

I sat down with her. "Mona really hit it off with Shirley."

A faint smile. "Did she?"

"Come on. I'll show you." There was no hiding it from her now that she was here, unless we spent the evening in the kitchen.

The dining room looked pretty good actually, kind of bright and bare with the carpet gone and the fresh paint. I could see now the crazy creativity in Mona's paint job that Dennis had seen and began thinking about leaving the walls alone. They shone in the overhead light, putting me in mind of abstract murals.

I took her into the living room. She peered around in the dim light of the floor lamp while I switched on the other lights. We'd torn that carpet out too, Mona and Shirley and I, and pitched it.

"Ta-da," I said, making a sweeping gesture at the walls.

"Who did this?" she asked.

I hesitated.

"Mona," she guessed. "What got into her?"

"I was on call, staying at Dennis and Nance's house over the weekend. She was home painting with a vengeance." I shrugged, feeling only fatalistic now that I was no longer angry. I watched Sally, trying to read her thoughts, and jumped when Shirley came into the room.

"I'm stuck in the driveway." Shirley looked shamefaced. "I got myself in deep. Is that your Chrysler van out there, Sally?"

Sally nodded.

"I doubt if you can get out either. Not till tomorrow anyway."

"I didn't bring my nightie," Sally said.

"Neither did I, and I'll bet Abby doesn't have one that'll fit me."

"I'll find something," I assured her, although I didn't think even my dad's old clothes would fit Shirley. "I guess you're staying to dinner."

I put the salmon under the broiler, the potatoes in the microwave, and the salad on the table. In fifteen minutes we sat down to eat.

VIII

Mona called during the meal to tell me she'd arrived and that they were sitting on the veranda in the warm evening. "Who's there?" she asked. "I hear voices."

"Shirley and Sally. Their cars are stuck in the driveway."

"I wish I was home." She sounded wistful.

"Why? We've got at least six inches of snow on the ground and it's still coming down. You got out of here just in time."

"You waited till I left and invited them to dinner, didn't you?"

"No," I said, although I'd invited Sally when I knew Mona was leaving. "Hey, you're the lucky one. I'm here in the cold, cleaning up after you. Let me talk to Mom."

"You couldn't wait for me to go, could you?" she hissed, and then Mom came on the line.

"Hi, honey. Are you snowed in?"

"Yes."

"It's lovely here. You can still come."

"I have to hang around till the work is done." I'd told her about Mona's paint job, and she and Dad had offered to pay for the work that had to be done. "Why don't I call you tomorrow? I've got company. We're all stuck here." Shirley was telling Sally about her decision to change her sex, and I wanted to hear.

Shirley glanced at me as I sat down again. "Did *you* guess?"

"Guess what?" I knew she was asking if I'd thought she was a man.

"About me. It's okay."

"Dennis told me."

"What did he say?"

"He said you were his best worker and that you hated wearing jeans."

Shirley threw back her head and laughed. If she shaved, it didn't show. "Did he say that technically I was still a he?"

"Yeah," I admitted, "but he said you'd make a beautiful woman."

She laughed again. "Ever since I can remember I wanted to be a girl."

"I always thought it was easier to be male. The clothes, the hair, the job scene," I interjected.

"I love women's clothes and long hair. I hate men's shoes and apparel and crew cuts."

"I prefer sweatpants," I said. "You're lucky you don't have to wear a suit and tie."

"I don't know if I could handle that. I'd rather wear a dress or a skirt, but it's hard to find women's clothes that fit. I wish I were petite like you two."

"How would you climb a ladder in a skirt?" Sally asked.

"Carefully." Shirley smiled. "I know it's not practical to wear anything but pants on my job."

"At least, you can reach the top cupboard," Sally said, handing Shirley a wineglass to put away. They were drying the wine glasses and pots and pans I'd washed after filling the dishwasher. "I think it takes a lot of guts to do what you're doing."

"So do I," I agreed.

"It wasn't so much a choice as something I felt I had to do. My parents are unhappy about it. I'm their only son."

That silenced me for a minute. I thought about my parents and wondered if they were disappointed with Mona and me, but their only son had reproduced. Maybe that was enough.

"Do you play poker?" Shirley asked, when the kitchen was clean.

I got a deck of cards out of the whatnot drawer and a box of poker chips. "I'm game."

"Me, too," Sally said.

Opening the bottle of white wine, I poured a round and sat at the table. Shirley took the cards and shuffled, fanning them, then set the deck down for me to cut. She had long fingers with square nails, a man's hands. Anyone studying them would look to her face for clarity.

"Five card stud, deuces wild." All business, she dealt the cards.

We played till we emptied the bottle of wine, until I ran out of chips. "I give up." I still had to change bedsheets. "I'll see what I can find for nightwear."

"Want some help?" Sally asked, getting up to follow.

"Sure." I tried to walk a straight line and stumbled on the stairs.

We changed Mona's sheets and put fresh ones on my parents' bed. Shirley appeared in the doorway of the bedroom as I looked through my dad's drawers for something to fit her.

"You're going to have to sleep in your undies, Shirley," I said, tucking the musty-smelling clothes back in the drawer. I'd have to run them through the washer. Dad's old bathrobe hung on a hook behind the door, but it looked much too small. "Try this on."

The bathrobe hugged Shirley's shoulders, the sleeves ending halfway up her forearms, the front gaping when she tied the cloth belt. I swallowed a laugh. "My father isn't very big."

Handing Sally a nightshirt I'd never worn, I gave them both towels and washcloths as well as two of the new toothbrushes Mona was always buying. She was obsessed with clean teeth.

When we went to bed, the wind no longer howled around the house. I looked out my window at the white lawn and felt the cold radiating through the glass. Tomorrow I'd have to fill the feeders. This time of year the birds ran short of food without any snow on the ground.

The phone rang in the night. I fumbled for it and moaned, "What?"

"I want to come home," Mona whined.

"Mona, I'm asleep. We're all asleep. I told Mom I'd call tomorrow." My thick tongue stuck to the roof of my mouth.

Her voice rose. "Shirley's sleeping there? She'll be gone when I get home. I'll never see her again."

"So?" I said.

"I really like her."

I scooted up on an elbow, knowing I had to thwart this infatuation. I told her Shirley was going to have a sex change operation, that she was still a he.

"I don't care," she said after a short silence. "I'll help her through it."

"Mona, go to bed. I can't talk about this right now." She'd wakened me from a drunken sleep. I closed my eyes against the pulsing beat in my head.

"Tell her not to finish before I get back."

"I can't do that."

"Please. I want to get to know her."

"Forget it. Forget her."

The rest of the conversation I failed to recall in the morning light, although I knew I'd talked to Mona and that it had something to do with Shirley. I lay quietly in the dazzling glare of sun reflecting painfully off snow, and squeezed my eyes shut. A terrible thirst consumed me, but I was reluctant to move my head off the pillow.

I might have stayed prone all day had I not heard movement out in the hall—Sally and Shirley talking. Failing to catch their words, I pushed myself up on my elbows, reached for the glass of water on the bedside table, and finished it off, then felt queasy.

Forcing myself to sit up, I let my feet fall to the floor. I so seldom drank any alcohol that I supposed I should consider myself lucky to feel as good as I did. Instead of pounding, my head felt as if it were stuffed with some kind of packing. Grabbing my robe off the back of a chair, I went out into the hall.

The voices were now downstairs, but I headed for the shower. Hot water on the outside and cold water inside. That was the remedy. The others had showered, their towels hung on the racks. I stuck my mouth under the faucet and drank.

Someone had made coffee. I smelled it as I made my way to the kitchen. Sally and Shirley looked up from the table. Mona would be jealous if she saw the two of them, hands cupped around steaming mugs, sharing a moment.

"Sleep all right?"

"Like the dead," they said in unison, then laughed.

I looked through the kitchen window at the drifted snow out back, at the birds devouring seed. "I see the good fairy filled the feeders."

Shirley laughed again, a sound that came from her depths. "That'd be me. I was checking on the truck, which is still very stuck."

"Thanks. Saved me having to fill them. What's it like out?"

"It's heavy snow. Who plows you out here? Do you have a snowblower?"

"One big enough to do the walk and driveway apron. The neighboring farmer should be by soon with his tractor and blade. Hungry? Want some breakfast?"

"I'll fix it. You sit down and drink your coffee," Sally said.

Collapsing in one of the chairs, I wondered why they looked so much better than I did. I'd seen my face in the mirror. White as paste with dark, bloody holes for eyes.

"Toast?" Sally's voice came from behind me.

"Please. Plain." I'd be lucky if I kept it down.

A tractor roared up the driveway. Shirley stood and pulled a jacket on. "I better go out and help."

The toast popped, and Sally put a hand on my shoulder as she set it in front of me on a small plate. "There you go." She poured more coffee and sat next to me. "You don't look so hot."

"I don't feel so good. I rarely drink when Mona's around." I forced a smile. "She called in the middle of the night, wanting to come home. She's fallen for Shirley."

Sally smiled a little. "It's sort of confusing, this sex change thing, especially when Shirley is sensitive and handsome and personable. You have to wonder if you're attracted to the man or the budding woman."

"You, too?" I asked, squinting at her.

"She exudes a certain magnetism. I felt it."

Surprised by jealousy, I looked away. "I didn't."

She put a hand on my arm, sending a jolt of pleasure right to my groin, the part of me I thought was dead. "You have it, too."

"Oh sure," I said. "I'm about as magnetic as a toad."

She didn't laugh. "Mona had it in high school. So much energy."

"That's a manifestation of bipolar disorder."

"It's something else with Shirley."

"She's not bipolar." I nibbled at the toast. "Do you have to go home?"

"Is Shirley going to stay and work?"

"She said she was. I can get something out of the freezer for supper." There were pizzas and leftover stew.

"Are you inviting me to dinner again?"

"Yes."

"You look like you should go back to bed."

I wondered what it would be like to go to bed with her. I should have asked Mona about Sally's love life, if she had one and with whom, but Mona would probably tell her.

She got up and went to the door. The tractor was still roaring outside. I followed. Together we peered at the snowy yard.

"I'm going out." I grabbed my jacket off the hook in the mu room. Perhaps the cold would make me feel better.

"Me, too."

We pulled on boots and stepped into an almost springlike wind. I remembered the sandhill cranes the last time she'd been here and wondered how they'd fared in the storm.

John Delancey was pulling the panel truck out of a snowbank. Squinting against the painful glare, I returned his wave.

"I better move the van. Good thing I don't have the BMW." Sally pulled keys out of her pocket. The snow a foot behind and around her vehicle had been removed, but the Chrysler sat in its own drift. She waded through it and climbed behind the wheel. By now the tractor was partway down the drive, towing the panel truck. Sally started the engine and spun the wheels back and forth. The van went nowhere. She got out and came back to me. "I guess it's too close to the ground."

The three of us pushed the Chrysler out of the drift. When the wheels caught firm ground, it shot backward and I fell up to my elbows in snow. Shirley hauled me out.

"You all right?"

"Yep. How much do I owe you, John?"

"You're not paying," Shirley protested.

"The usual," John said.

"I'll write a check. Thanks so much."

After John left and we went inside, Shirley said disconsolately, "John thought I was a man."

I'd have thought so, too, all bundled up like she was, because of her size.

"Did you tell him your name?" Sally asked.

"Nope."

"How do you know what he thought and why do you care?" I said.

"It's so hard to explain." Shirley's hair was blown, her cheeks red. "I feel so self-conscious sometimes. I wonder if I'll still feel that way after the operation?"

"You're beautiful," Sally said.

Shirley smiled. "Am I? Would you think I was a woman?"

"That's the mystery." Sally could talk circles around anything.

Looking puzzled, Shirley repeated, "Mystery? I've spent a fortune on hormone therapy."

"It's how you feel about yourself that counts," I said. "Are you having second thoughts?"

"I'm not going back to being a man," she told us.

"Well, that's that," I said. "The only way to go is forward."

Shirley put both hands on the table. "I better get to work."

"No. I'm not up to crawling around the floor today."

"You don't have to. I just want to get started on the living room."

"I think you should take a couple days off," I said.

Shirley looked from me to Sally. "You staying?" she asked Sally.

Sally glanced at me. "For a while."

"Okay. I'll be here Monday." Shirley got up and pushed her chair in. "Thanks for the bed and breakfast."

"Hey, it's the least I can do." I'd given her a key to the house. She was usually here before I got home from work.

IX

Left alone, silence fell over us. I wondered why I'd asked her to stay when all I really wanted to do was put my head on the kitchen table and sleep. In the quiet, broken only by public radio's *Classics by Request* playing from the radio on the kitchen counter, Sally picked up a section of the unread Saturday paper I'd fetched from the end of the driveway.

The phone rang shrilly. "Damn," I said, knowing who it was.

The machine picked up after four rings. "It's me. Mona. Answer the phone, Abby. I know you're snowed in." Then I heard her call Mom.

"Hi, sweetheart. We finally get one of you down here and she wants to come home."

I snatched the receiver off the wall. "Don't let her, Mom. Tell her anything, but keep her there."

"Ha, you are there. I knew it. I want to talk to Shirley." All our voices—Mom's, Mona's, and mine spilled into the room.

"Shirley left. She won't be back till Monday."

"Give me her phone number or I'm hopping on the next plane."

"I'll find out and let you know." Dennis would have it. "You okay, Mom?"

"What's going on? Who's Shirley? A new friend?"

"A very nice woman trapped in a man's body. Mona wants to know her better." I knew this would stump my mother, who, although kind, was rather conventional.

"Oh. How can she be a she if she's still a he?"

"Well, she's had hormone therapy, which has given her breasts and taken away facial and body hair. On the surface, she looks like both."

"I've heard of things like this. I just never knew anyone like that firsthand."

"Well, you still don't, Mom, and probably never will." Unless, of course, Shirley and Mona hooked up.

"Are you alone?"

"No. I have a friend here. I'll get Shirley's number." If I were Shirley, I'd run like hell if Mona started pursuing me.

Sally was looking at me. "She wants to see Shirley bad enough to come home?"

I nodded and rang Dennis's number. Nance answered.

"Is Dennis there, Nance?"

"No hello, how are you? Where are your manners?"

"Gone. I need Shirley's phone number. Mona is going to come home if she can't talk to her."

"The Shirley that was Shawn?" Surprise edged her voice.

"She's very nice, Nance. So nice that Mona fell for her."

"I thought Mona was straight. Wasn't she always bringing home men?"

"Don't remind me," I snapped. "Now can I talk to Dennis?"

"You don't need to take that tone." She called Dennis.

In a moment, he came on the line. "What's this about Mona having a crush on Shirley?"

"If I don't give her Shirley's number, she's coming home. She just left here yesterday."

He gave me the number and asked, "How's Shirley getting along with the work?"

"She's doing a great job."

"Are you snowed in?"

"Not anymore. John plowed us out." I said good-bye and hung up.

Sally looked up from the newspaper. "Did you get the number?"

I nodded. "Bear with me while I call Mona."

"Take your time."

After playing a few games of cribbage, we went outside to walk up and down the driveway. The road was too sloppy to tackle. Birds sang as clumps of snow fell from the trees and eaves.

"I was in Mona's wedding with you." Sally wrapped her jacket tightly around her to keep out the damp wind. "I liked Douglas. He was my dentist till he moved away."

I barely remembered her at the wedding. "Douglas was okay. Mona got him into some tough financial situations." I half-turned to look at her. "I don't blame him for wanting out. My last roommate, who came with me when I moved back home, couldn't handle Mona either." Sometime I'd show her my bedroom walls. Then she'd understand that Lisa had been more than a roommate.

Long purple shadows crossed the snow. The wind died while we walked the drive, talking. A chill settled over the landscape—and me.

"Let's go inside." The fresh air had cleared my head. I thought I could handle a drink or two. Isn't that what people downed to cure a hangover?

She fixed drinks while I got a large pizza out of the freezer and doctored it with peppers and onions, then tore up lettuce for a salad.

"Sure this isn't going to knock you out?" Sally asked, putting a glass in front of me.

"We'll see." I took a sip and set it down. "Good. Thanks."

"Anything else I can do?"

"Tell me about yourself."

"I've been so busy these past years that there isn't much to tell. If you're going to make it as an attorney, you put in a lot of hours. I usually spend at least one day of the weekend in the office. This has been a real respite for me."

"Maybe you should stay tomorrow, too, then."

She laughed and looked away. "I don't think so."

"I love your smile," I blurted, and blushed.

She appeared startled and concentrated on her glass, which she turned around and around between slender fingers.

This was going nowhere. She was probably straight as a stick and I wasn't tuned in. I never asked or admitted to anything, either. I let people make their own assumptions.

Clearing her throat, she said, "I've had a very nice time. Would you come for dinner at my house next Friday? Mona's welcome, too, if she's home."

"You bet I'll come." I'd been wondering when she was going to invite me over. "But Mona won't be home till a week from Sunday, unless she decides to return early to see Shirley." Whenever I thought nothing could surprise me anymore, something would. Mona shooting at me, the painted woodwork, her falling for Shirley. These were things I expected from clients, not my sister, although Mona could have been a client.

The windows turned dark with night as we ate the pizza. "You've been here this long, you might as well stay one more night," I said. "The roads are probably still slick."

"I need to change clothes," she said.

"I can lend you some of mine. You look about the same size." Actually, she was a little taller and fuller.

"Okay. I'd rather drive home during daylight."

I smiled, pleased at her acquiescence, hoping she liked my company as much as I liked hers. She was peaceful.

Before we went to bed, I showed her my bedroom. "Mona painted this mural. It drove Lisa away," I said, trying to read her face.

She studied it as if it were a piece of art. "It's quite good, actually. She does have talent."

"What a way to use it. I think I'm going to leave the paint on the downstairs walls as is."

"I would. It's interesting." She looked at the naked ladies a little longer. "You must like this too."

"I do. Sort of."

"I guess I'll go to bed. Have you got something I can read?"

I wanted in the worst way to ask her to sleep with me, but I couldn't say the words. Nor did she. "Sure. Take your pick." The two bookcases in my room were packed with recent novels.

"Is this good?" she asked, picking out *The Dive from Clausen's Pier*.

"Yes, but not funny. *Good in Bed* is both." I was always buying books. I'd take them to bed and fall asleep reading.

I missed her as soon as she closed Mona's door behind her. Climbing into bed alone, I realized how much I wanted a comforting presence to lie beside me. The naked ladies were patterned with shadows. They were my companions. "Fondle me," I whispered to the pair who were exchanging caresses, but, of course, I had to touch myself, which I found so boring, I soon lost interest.

Around three in the morning the phone rang. Damn, I thought, dragging myself toward the receiver. I should have taken it off the hook. It was work calling wanting to know what to do with Karl Jankowski who had been taken to ER after being spotted leaning on the railing of the College Avenue bridge, so drunk he could barely stand.

"Put him in detox," I said. After last time, I didn't dare suggest jail. I couldn't risk his going into DTs again.

I lay awake a long time after the phone call, screwing my eyes shut, unable to stop my brain from tossing things around. Like Karl, most of our clients were not going to make useful citizens. They were either unmotivated or too sick. With little money they were shut out of the regular system.

I awoke to birdsong and opened my eyes to sunshine. Getting up, I trotted down the hall to the bathroom. Sally's door was shut. It was only six-thirty. I tried to sleep again and couldn't. Going downstairs, I started the coffee, then pulled on a jacket and walked to the end of the driveway to retrieve the Sunday paper.

The warm breath of spring was in the air, melting the snow, causing the birds to go crazy with song. I drank coffee and read the paper until Sally appeared, showered and dressed in the jeans and long-sleeved shirt I'd loaned her. *Weekend Edition* aired on public radio.

"Thanks for the clothes."

"They fit well." She filled them out nicely. I thought she looked sexy.

"Have you been to the PAC?" The new Performing Arts Center. I was perusing the lifestyle section.

"Yes. Have you?"

"I went to *Mama Mia* with Nance and Dennis," I said, revealing my bleak social life. "Would you like to see *The Producers?*"

"I would."

"I'll get tickets," I said.

"Let me give you some money." She poured herself a cup of coffee.

"You can pay me after I get the tickets." The twinge of guilt I felt for not including Mona vanished quickly. She could ask Shirley.

Sally left after breakfast. Experiencing an attack of unexpected loneliness as the van disappeared from sight, I reminded myself that this was what I wanted—to be alone.

X

On Monday when I walked into the phone room where the crisis unit held their staff meetings, the chatter shifted to include me. We had continuing personal discussions about family matters, friends, car problems, house maintenance, vacations, pets, cottages.

"Were you snowed in?" Debbie asked.

"I was."

"We took the kids sledding at Reed Park." This from Bob.

"We got out the cross-country skis," Mark said.

"We sat around and watched TV," Debbie admitted. "What's it like without Mona?"

"A little lonely," I said with surprise, realizing I already missed her.

Between the meetings and clients the day sped by. When I walked out to my car, the sun shone down from a cloudless sky and only a few piles of snow remained on the ground.

I found Shirley on a ladder in the living room, slapping paint remover on the wood. She looked down at me.

"Has Mona called you yet?" I asked.

"Only night and day," she said with a grin.

"I'm sorry. She said she'd come home if I didn't give her your number." It occurred to me that Mona hadn't called me since I'd given her Shirley's phone number.

"Dennis told me. Hey, it's okay. I like talking to her."

"Are you serious?"

"I am."

"Why don't you have dinner with me?" She was beginning to feel like family

"I don't want to take advantage."

"You're not," I said. I owed her something for passing on her number to Mona.

The week whizzed by. Sally and I had changed our lunch dates to Thursdays, which was when she reminded me that I was invited to her house for dinner on Friday. As if I would have forgotten.

"What can I bring?" I'd already decided on a good wine.

"Yourself. It's all taken care of." One corner of her mouth quirked upward. I smiled back, my heart pumping a little faster. "Have you heard from Mona?"

"Nope. She's calling Shirley instead."

The same guy who always waited on us filled our coffee cups. "How are you ladies today? Do you want the usual? Soup and bread?"

"Yep," we said in unison, and he went off with a skip in his step.

"You have to admire him," I said, noticing the sway in his tight little bottom. "He's so cocksure about his sexuality." I thought I saw slight amusement in her eyes. "Mona's coming home Sunday. Guess who's going to meet her at the airport?"

Her light brown eyebrows lofted. "Shirley?"

I nodded.

"They must derive comfort from one another."

I'd given a lot of thought to their mutual attraction. "They're both different. They don't fit in." I leaned back in my chair. "Mona's lonely. Her friends have shied away. She's been divorced seven years, and as far as I know, no one's on the horizon." I was lonely too and had no one on the horizon either, unless Sally was peering my way. I couldn't read her.

On the way back to the office I thought about my conversation with Mom the previous evening. She'd said Mona talked to Shirley a lot. I supposed I should be grateful Mona wasn't waking me up nights, but I even kind of missed that.

At work I avoided the elevator, as usual, and climbed the back stairs with Tracy. "How's Anna?" I knew she'd been released from the hospital. She was included in the med runs.

"Her daughter might take her in."

"Is that good?"

"I don't know. They have an off-and-on-again relationship."

I'd talked to her daughter briefly. The woman had seemed distraught, caught between her mother's needs and her children's. It wasn't an unusual situation.

In my office, I glanced at my appointment book. I'd scribbled Elizabeth Howard for one o'clock. It wasn't a name I knew. I went out to the reception area. The woman who looked up from the magazine was in her early thirties, pale and scared. I recognized her.

"Come in, Elizabeth." I smiled through my surprise. She followed me down the hallway, and I closed the door behind us. I shook and held her hand. "Elizabeth Halbertson. Right?" She had lost weight. Her right arm was in a sling.

Her smile trembled. "I'm changing my name. He'll get out, you know, and come looking for me."

If he got out, he surely would do just that, but I didn't want to fuel her fear. "Have a seat." I nodded at the sling. "How are you recovering?"

"He shot me in the shoulder." She clutched a worn black purse in her lap. "He's gonna kill me."

I looked in her eyes, wide and blue, and wondered what to say. I knew the judge had set Brume's bond at fifty thousand dollars. "Have you tried the battered women's shelter?" Its location was supposedly secret.

"He seemed so interested in me at first. You know? He wanted to be with me all the time. He said he wanted me all to himself. After a while, I couldn't go anywhere without him. He didn't like my friends or my family. Then he began accusing me of seeing men behind his back." She looked at me beseechingly. "I tried to leave him, but he wouldn't let me go. He said he'd kill himself. Then he said he'd kill me."

It was an old story. Women who were unsure of their attractiveness were easy prey for men like Brume. "I'll keep tabs on Brume. If they're going to release him, I'll get you into the battered women's shelter. You might have to find another job. He knows where you work, I assume."

She nodded, her fingers working the fabric of her purse. "It's not so easy to get another job."

"I know. Where are you working?"

"In Shopko at the checkout counter."

"Maybe you can find work that's not so public." I knew this woman must have a myriad of problems to discuss.

Anger simmered to the surface. "Why should I have to hide from him? Why won't anyone protect me? I know the police won't. I got that restraining order, and what good did it do? He shot me."

"There'll be a trial, you know. Your testimony will be important."

Terror flashed across her face. "I can't," she gasped. She was fidgety the rest of the hour. She reminded me of deer that went a little crazy during the hunting sesson, only worse. She knew she'd be pursued.

When she left, we'd just begun to scrape away the layers of her life. Her father had been much like Brume, maybe not violent, but controlling. She made an appointment for the following week.

XI

Sally lived on the river in a house built into a hill. Grasses and plants were only beginning to climb through last year's growth. Birds feasted at the feeders hanging from the trees. Flotillas of geese and ducks swam past. Screaming gulls flew over the water.

We ate on the sunporch facing the river with the windows cracked open, so that we could hear the birds. The focus was on the backyard and river. The windows that faced the street were closed and covered with blinds.

For hors d'oeuvres, she'd wrapped mozzarella cheese and sun dried tomatoes in grape leaves, brushed them with olive oil, and grilled them on the wood deck after my arrival. The vodka was Svedka from Sweden. I tried not to wolf down the appetizers and slug back the liquor.

Dinner was a dish made with dark noodles, onions, red peppers, carrots, sliced and grated lettuces, with a peanut butter based sauce. The dry red wine was my offering. I pushed the last of the sauce around my plate with a piece of fresh wheat bread.

"There's dessert," she said. "Key lime pie."

Although uncomfortably full, I managed to eat a piece. "You must like to cook."

"I do, when I have the time."

I helped her clean up. Searching for a way to bring up Elizabeth Halbertson without naming her, I asked, "Are you familiar with James Brume?"

"Yes." She gave me a measured gaze.

"Do you have any idea how long a sentence he might get?"

"Charlie Neff set a high bail."

"Yes." Neff was one of the judges I really liked.

"He hands down stiff sentences."

"How stiff?"

"In the past he's come down hard on abusers."

"Could Brume be out in a year or two? Could he get probation?"

"I don't think so. There's truth in sentencing now, you know."

I did know, but that sometimes made judges more lenient than the days when good behavior could get a prisoner out early. Brume was pleading not guilty by reason of insanity. A savvy psychiatrist would find him to be antisocial, a danger to society, but perfectly sane. I would probably have to testify because I'd seen him in jail. It left me feeling oddly unsafe and, therefore, easily able to empathize with Elizabeth Halbertson.

"Did Shirley finish the living room?"

"She'll be done by the weekend." The removal of the stain and the carpeting had taken years off the place. Shirley had become a fixture in the house—there when I came home from work, staying to have a drink with me, sometimes lingering for dinner. She was good company. I'd miss her.

"I should tell you my partner has agreed to defend Brume," Sally said quietly. "I can't really talk about the case."

Shocked, I stammered, "But I thought you only handled civil cases."

"Don wants to get into defense. It was his idea to defend Brume. That's all I can say about it."

I wanted to argue, to rail against this decision. How could a self-respecting attorney defend a scumbag like Brume? "He's physically and emotionally abusive, you know. Women should use him for target practice."

She gave me another look that told me to put a lid on it. "Everyone's entitled to a good legal defense."

"I'm sure Elizabeth Halbertson would agree," I said sarcastically. If he killed Elizabeth when he got out in a few years, could anyone justify the good legal defense that gave him a lighter sentence? Would Elizabeth get police protection when he was out? Of course not. My heart hammered with indignation against the law that protected a man like Brume and punished his victim, but I said nothing.

"I'm not the enemy," Sally told me gently, her eyes grave, and I calmed down some. "I never said the law is fair. It's supposed to be equal."

"Well, it isn't, is it? The rich get the best counsel, the poor get the dregs."

She lifted a shoulder somewhat resignedly. "Brume is poor," she pointed out, "but the law is made and enforced by people, so what can you expect."

She was right, of course. The laws could only be as good as those who made and defended them. If Janssen got a light sentence for Brume, it would be good advertising for his and Sally's law firm, probably luring richer clients their way.

"Can't you keep Janssen from taking the case?"

"He agreed to do it." She looked me square in the eyes—mine angry, hers sad—and I saw it was no use arguing with her.

We went to her living room, a small parlor adjacent to the sunporch. By now it was dark outside. Through the slightly open windows we heard a heron squawk down by the river.

"Such an elegant bird, such an ugly sound."

I still seethed with anger and only nodded.

"Can I get you anything?" she asked.

"Water would be nice." While she was gone to get it, I picked up a magazine and glanced through it, trying to banish the image of Elizabeth Halbertson clutching her purse.

"Want to see the rest of the house?" she asked, returning to the room and handing me an ice filled glass.

"Sure."

The rooms were small, but the many windows, the overhead fan lights, the oak floors, and very little clutter gave the place an airy, open feeling. We stalled in her sparsely furnished bedroom. The sleigh bed was covered with a homemade quilt. Books lay everywhere—piled on the floor, the bed tables, the three bookcases.

The den also held myriads of books, along with a desk and computer and a comfortable-looking chair under a table lamp.

"You read a lot," I said when we returned to the living room. That, at least, we held in common.

"Don't hold this case against me," she said. "It wasn't my idea. I despise men like Brume."

I shrugged dismissively. "It's your business, not mine." That was the problem, of course. She was the senior partner. Surely she had some control over the cases they took.

I left shortly after, troubled, driving home under a sky cluttered with stars. The house was dark, and I turned on lights as I entered. I felt lonelier than ever. I would welcome Mona's return Sunday night.

Shirley showed up Saturday morning around nine for some finishing touches. "I slept in," she said apologetically. "Mona likes to call in the middle of the night."

I smiled. How well I knew. "She doesn't sleep much."

"She's so alive, isn't she?" Shirley looked at me expectantly.

"She's bipolar," I said, feeling a rush of guilt as if I'd disclosed a secret.

"I know. She told me."

I doubted if Shirley knew what being bipolar was all about.

"She makes me feel special. I used to be the odd person out.

You know? I guess I still am, but she thinks I'm just great for some reason." She smiled sheepishly.

"You are," I assured her, and she looked embarrassed.

"You must wonder about us," she said, concentrating on what she was doing.

"I suppose you're just good friends." I hoped that was true. Mona needed all the friends she could get.

She cleared her throat. "Well, it's more than that. We have so much to say to each other."

I found out how much more than friends they were when Shirley returned with Mona from the airport. Tanned and sparkling, Mona talked animatedly, while Shirley nodded and smiled.

"You have to go for a visit, Abby. I'll be just fine now that Shirley's here," she said.

When they disappeared into Mona's bedroom, the full implication of what she'd said dawned on me. Shirley had come to stay. I was dumbfounded. Was the sex change operation off? Had they decided to become lovers?

Lying in my bed, I was tempted to call Sally. If Mona could have Shirley, I wanted someone. I lay in bed, listening for sounds from the room across the hall. The naked ladies taunted me from the shadows.

XII

Shirley left early the next morning, leaving me alone with Mona. I hardly knew what to say that wouldn't incur her wrath and took the plunge after a deep breath.

"Are you and Shirley lovers?"

Mona frowned. "Give me one good reason why I should answer that?"

She had no qualms when questioning me about my life. "One of you is going to be hurt." What was she thinking? How could a relationship between her and Shirley work? I squeezed my coffee cup between both hands.

"We're adults." She tossed her hair, which had turned redder in the Arizona sun.

"You're straight, and Shirley's going to have a sex change operation." Of course, she knew these things, but I was exasperated.

"Maybe, maybe not."

"She's not going to have a sex change? Or you're not straight?"

She snapped, "Stop trying to run my life."

I left for work, wondering whether my meddling was based on concern for Mona's best interests or mine.

Before staffing, Debbie asked, "Is Mona back?"

I nodded. "It looks like Shirley's moving in with us. She spent the night in Mona's room." Three pairs of eyes homed in on me. "Well? What's your take on this? Should I be worried or pleased? Should I butt out of Mona's business as she wants me to do?"

"Reminds me of a book I read where a woman leaves her husband for another man who then turns around and gets a sex change operation, leaves her and eventually ends up with the ex-husband," Bob said.

"Only you, Bob, would come up with a book to fit the situation," Debbie pointed out.

I waited for Mark to say something.

He looked deep in thought. Finally, he said, "I suppose Mona has found a best friend in the *woman* Shirley along with a physical attraction to the *man* Shirley still is, if that makes any sense." Actually, it sounded a lot like what Sally had said when Mona had first expressed an interest in Shirley.

Mark always exhibited empathy for the most bizarre of our clients and felt real pain for the hopelessly mentally ill. He was around my age, married with teenage boys. The rumors that swirled around our halls somehow passed unnoticed by him.

Debbie was a friend to most of the staff. She chatted with them about their personal lives. She was older than me by three years and had two grown children. Like me she was a little burned out by the job and tended to regard our clients with a slightly jaded eye.

Bob, who was still in his thirties, was eclectic and avid in his interests. He viewed life as his two young daughters did—ever changing, always interesting. He had great sympathy for our clients and found working with them both challenging and rewarding.

"You're probably right. We'll see how long this lasts." I sat on the couch next to Debbie.

After staffing, I went back to my office to catch up on e-mail. I had a meeting at ten. The phone rang as soon as I sat down in front of the computer. Absently, I picked it up.

"Abby? It's Sally. Can you come over after work?"

It beat going home to Mona and Shirley. "It's my turn to have you over," I said. I'd thanked her for the meal by phone on Saturday. She hadn't asked me over then.

"Just come. Please?"

"Okay." I'd planned to call Dennis, to maybe go over to his house. I wanted to talk to him.

"If you go home first, bring something to wear to work tomorrow, your toothbrush, and your nightie." Her voice sounded different—strained, a little quivery.

I stammered, "Okay," wondering if we were finally getting it on.

The day plodded by, despite meetings and clients. I was gathering up my things to go when Tracy showed up at the open door of my office just before five o'clock.

She knocked on the frame. "Got a minute?" she asked with a tentative smile.

I set my purse and appointment book down. "Sure. What's up?"

"It's Anna. I'm worried about her. She thinks her daughter wants to kill her."

"Nothing new about that. Is she off her meds?" I pictured Anna, her white hair, her blue eyes. She was once a beautiful woman, I was sure.

"I don't know. I think her care might be just too much for the daughter. She loses her temper."

"Should we put her in a crisis bed?"

"I think she'd be very unhappy anywhere but in her own apartment."

"Then we're back to square one."

"A room with a bath, if we can find one. Her daughter promises to look in on her, and, of course, we'd monitor her meds."

"Good. See what you can do. I think we might have a bed at the

Providence House." It was one of the county-run facilities that offered rooms to the mentally ill. "Anna will probably think everyone's trying to kill her there, too, though," I warned Tracy, "and she'll have a roommate."

"I know. If we can just keep her medicated, she'll be okay."

I drove out to the house to get some clothes and overnight necessities. Mona and Shirley were sitting on the living room couch, her small hand lost in Shirley's large one, her head on Shirley's broad shoulder. I flew past them and up the stairs with a hello, hoping to get out of there without a conversation.

I put my book, my sleep shirt, clean underwear and knee highs, and grooming necessities in my overnight bag. I placed the shirt and slacks for work tomorrow over the zipped top, and slung it all over my left shoulder. Smiling at the naked ladies, I left the room.

"I'm going to stay in town overnight," I said on my way out. "I've got things to do."

Before Shirley, Mona would have grilled me on the details. Now she just said, "Okay." It occurred to me that she might be glad to have me gone.

Shirley took my bag away. "I'll carry this out."

I took one glance at the living room and thought how nice it looked because of her. The berber carpet and the off-white strangely painted walls lent light. Even the old furniture fit with the decor.

Outside, the air was soft, springlike. I touched Shirley's arm. "I love the way the house looks."

"Thanks," she said in her deep voice. The large Adam's apple bobbed. "Mona said you were upset this morning."

I met her clear gaze, and sighed. "She's straight, and you're planning a sex change operation. How is that going to work?"

"We'll have to see," she said earnestly. "I hope it does. Nobody has ever made me feel so good."

I slid behind the driver's wheel. I was excited about what the evening might hold for me. Still, I couldn't resist saying, "Yeah, well, wait until she starts spending money."

Shirley closed the car door and talked to me through the open window. "It's not like we're getting married."

I bit my tongue, turned the Saturn around, and sped off toward town. Sunlight fell across fields of alfalfa and winter wheat. The deep frost of a dry, cold winter hadn't killed their roots. In the ditches red-winged blackbirds shrilled. They would weave their nests around the grasses when they grew tall enough. It was April. Snow could still fall. Frost would surely cover the new growth. Gardeners didn't plant till Memorial Day. Farmers usually put their corn and soybeans in the ground before the end of May.

I opened the window and sniffed at the air. Crossing a creek I listened for frogs and was rewarded with a croak or two. I would have to wait another month for their discordant concert. The birds were tuning up for the mating season.

I glanced at my watch, wondering if there was still time to stop by and talk to Dennis, and punched his number on my cell phone.

"Dennis, it's me, Abby. I wanted to talk to you about Shirley."

"What about Shirley? I'm on my way out."

"She's moved in with us, with Mona."

"What? I thought she'd finished the work."

"She did. She and Mona really hit it off."

"They're doing the dirty?" he asked.

I couldn't stop a grin. "Looks that way."

"Very odd," he said. I heard the car start, his radio come on, the garage door opening, him backing out. "You want me to say something to her?"

"No, no. I just wanted to hear your thoughts."

"Well, I thought Shawn was nuts to want to be Shirley in the first place. Maybe she'll change her mind and stop this hormone business."

"I don't think so. I'm worried about my sister." If she lost Shirley, Mona was likely to spiral into depression. It would fall on me to take care of her.

"I have to meet the electrician at the building site. Why don't you buzz on over? We can talk when the electrician leaves."

"I don't have time. I'm going to a friend's house. Sally Shields. She's an attorney and on the zoning board."

"The name sounds familiar. Maybe I'd have to see her."

"Look, I'll talk to you later. Give my love to Nance." I'd strayed over the center line, and the truck I'd just missed blared its horn. My heart pounded out of sync. "I can't drive and talk on the phone at the same time."

"Okay, kiddo. Have a good time. Is this a date or what?"

"I don't know." I hung up.

XIII

I parked in the driveway at Sally's. A Lincoln Continental hugged the curb space. Sally opened the door, smiling and frowning at the same time if that's possible.

"My partner . . ." she said, gesturing toward the parlor. "Come in and meet him."

I followed her into the living room, glad I hadn't brought in my overnight bag.

"Don Janssen, Abby Dean," she said.

Janssen rose to his six feet plus and leaned forward to shake my hand. "I should be going." He was a handsome man, lean and muscular with a strong chin and close-set eyes. "Do I know you?"

"Maybe you've seen me around the courthouse. I work for the county. In mental health."

"Perhaps." But he looked uncertain. There was a resemblance between Mona and me. I expected that's what he saw. He glanced at Sally. "I'll see you at work, Sally. It was nice to meet you, Ms. Dean."

"Abby," I said. "Nice to meet you, too," I said to his back as Sally walked him to the front door.

She returned with a worried look. "Where's your nightie?"

"Tucked away in my bag in the car." I was standing near a window, staring at the river. Ducks and geese and gulls bobbed on the surface. I turned and looked into her dark eyes, stifling a sudden urge to laugh at the seriousness of her expression.

"Don was here to talk about Brume's defense. Apparently, Brume is not a likeable guy."

"Tell me something I don't know." I imagined Janssen trying to talk to Brume about his defense and Brume hopping mad because he still thought he was blameless. Brume had probably told Janssen that Elizabeth would never have been shot if the police hadn't gotten involved.

"Would you like a drink?"

"Some of that good Svedka vodka with tonic and a twist of lime if you've the makings." We were both still standing.

I followed her into the kitchen where she put the bottles on the counter, filled two glasses with ice, and set them down in front of me.

"I'll have the same," she said, slicing cheese and arranging it with crackers on a plate.

I made the drinks, and she led me to the porch where we'd eaten a few days ago. "I called you because I thought the other night ended badly. I don't want you angry with me."

"We're not on the same side. I'm cheering for Elizabeth Halbertson. You're defending James Brume." I took a swig of my drink and munched on a cracker.

A frown furrowed the space between her eyes.

I said, "Look, I don't want to argue either. Let's forget the Brumes and Halbertsons of the world." I wanted to leave work behind me.

"How are Mona and Shirley?" she asked as if searching for some topic of conversation.

I sighed. "All wrapped up in each other. Literally. Let's not talk about them, either." I could see her wondering what we would talk about. "How was your day?"

She laughed, startling me. "I thought we weren't going to talk about work." She sat in a rocker and began to eat and drink absently, staring out the window at the ever-moving river. "See the woodchuck down on the rocks?"

It was standing on its hind legs, balancing on its short furry tail, looking as if it were enjoying the view. I smiled. "Cute."

"I tried to grow an herb garden down there. Hog and the rabbits ate it all. That's what I call him"—she nodded at the woodchuck—"Hog for groundhog."

"Do you ever want to just quit everything and move to a place where you grow your own food and cut your own wood for heat, where there's no cable, no nearby shopping malls?" When work or Mona overwhelmed me, I thought along those lines.

I knew I wasn't a candidate for survival without the amenities, though. I'd hated weeding my parents' garden—the biting bugs, the stooping, the heat. I knew how to can tomatoes and beans but disliked the intense, boring labor associated with it. With vegetables, as with fruit, you had to work your ass off to turn the brief bounty into something you could store.

As for shooting game, I'd killed a squirrel on my first hunt, dropped the gun, and stumbled away, wailing. My dad shouted praises at my back. When I got home, I buried my face between my mother's breasts and wept. Mona and Craig, of course, had loved hunting with Dad. The quickest way to food was the one I took—the route to the grocery store or a restaurant.

She looked at me thoughtfully, as if she were taking me seriously. "Actually, I own a little piece of property on a trout stream. There's a small cabin on it."

The concept had immediate appeal—Sally and me, alone, two survivors in the wilderness. I knew reality was another thing altogether, though.

"I've always wondered if I could live off the land and what that would be like."

"Hard work," I told her.

"You've done it?"

Outside, the late afternoon sun gilded the crests of waves stirred up by the mild wind. The open windows let in the odor of water and earth. "We had a garden when I was young. My mom and I canned; my dad, Mona, and my brother hunted game. We raised chickens, too, which we ate." I remembered how they'd flopped around, the blood pumping out of their necks, after my dad cut off their heads—as if they didn't know they were dead. A reflexive action. I always swore I'd never eat them, but I had. Hunger had gotten the best of me.

"I don't think I could kill anything."

"Oh, I know I can't, unless it's a bug." I told her about shooting the squirrel, how I'd felt when it somersaulted in the air, then quivered before lying still. The squirrel personalized death, even more than the chickens, because I'd done the killing. Even though the squirrel would have been long dead from natural causes, I felt sad all over again that I'd caused its demise.

She looked at me as if seeing me anew. "I've never shot a gun. Maybe Mona would give me lessons. Or you."

"I don't like wild game," I said, as if we were seriously considering trying survival together. "Why don't you tell me why you asked me to stay overnight?" Heat rushed to my face.

"I thought it was better you stayed rather than drive home after a few drinks."

"Good thinking," I said, surprised by disappointment.

"Would you like another drink?" she asked.

I looked at mine in surprise. It was nearly empty. "Might as well."

I stayed put and watched Hog watching the river. Sally came back in a few minutes with fresh drinks.

"We're going to make our own pizza," she said. "How does that sound?"

"Like fun."

≈≈≈

When we sat down to eat, I asked her if she would really consider the radical lifestyle change we'd talked about, and confessed, "It's just a fantasy of mine that crops up when I'm fed up with things. I know I'm not suited for it."

"Not alone I wouldn't," she said, "nor would I sell the house. I'd rent it, just in case the survival experiment failed."

"And the law firm? You work long hours, weekends."

"Well, there are e-mail, telephones, fax machines. I'd drive into town when I had to go to court."

"You really were serious, weren't you?"

She shrugged. "Like you said, it's all talk. And you? Could you work from somewhere else?"

"No. I see clients every day, and I'm on call overnight once a month and one weekend twice a year." I leaned on my forearms. "I might come back to no job. I'm fed up with Mona and Shirley, is all."

"I see." She sounded disappointed.

"We have a garden now, you know—tomatoes, beans, cabbage, squash. We don't can anymore, though."

"Would you like to see the cabin?"

"I'd love to."

We drove there the following Saturday, saving me from a weekend of witnessing Mona and Shirley's open displays of affection. They pawed each other. I thought if I heard one more smacking kiss, I'd scream.

I'd never seen Mona so deliriously happy, and Shirley seemed equally enamored. Their misplaced passion baffled me. Nothing in my training or experience had prepared me for their romance. They not only called each other cutesy names, like honey bun and sweetmeat, but referred to each other in the third person. "Would sweet pea like a cup of coffee?" I found myself sarcastically mouthing answers like, "Does cutie pie want a kick in the ass?"

Sally picked me up in the BMW around nine. We were stopping at McDonald's for breakfast on the way out of town. I threw my bag in the back next to Sally's leather satchel and a cooler, and climbed into the luxurious leather passenger seat. We were staying overnight.

I ordered the eggs, bacon, and cheese bagel meal. Sally chose an egg McMuffin and three pancakes. The sun, flowing through the windows, covered us with a warm blanket. A fly buzzed against the glass.

"Tell me about the cabin," I said.

"There are some amenities, like running water and electricity, an indoor toilet, a shower, a basic kitchen, a table, chairs, beds. You'll see. I had the plumbers refill the water system. In the fall they drain the pipes and hot water heater. No TV, but there's a radio."

The temperature hovered around sixty when we climbed back into the low-slung car. Not warm enough to open the top. The radio, tuned to National Public Radio, played Sibelius's *Finlandia*. I fell asleep and only awakened when Sally turned onto a sandy, bumpy road.

"We're almost there," she said, giving me a smile.

"I'm sorry to be such rotten company, but I was awake half the night." Kept that way by the sounds emanating from Mona's bedroom, I could have added. Finally, I'd resorted to wearing earplugs. By then, though, I was so annoyed it took me another hour to go to sleep.

Sand roiled around us. At an opening in the pines, Sally turned and bounced up a barely discernable driveway—two dirt tracks with grass in between. We came to a stop at the top of a rise.

Set amidst gigantic white pines stood a small dark green cottage. I got out of the BMW, stiff from the drive, and walked with Sally toward the cabin. Spotting the trout stream, carving its way through banks of grasses and willow trees at the bottom of the hill, I stopped to look.

Trout streams are swift and cold and the color of tea. Drawn to the rushing water, I started down a series of sandy steps held in place by staked four-by-fours. Pine needles lay thick underfoot, dry and slippery. Along the stream the ground was soft. A rope hung from the branch of a stunted willow of immense girth.

"That's to swing on over the stream and drop in." Sally stood next to me, waving away a cloud of gnats. "It has to be really hot out. The water's icy."

"Sure is pretty, though." On the other side a forest of mixed trees climbed another hill. "Are there trout in here?"

"Yes. It's barbless season right now, though. Catch and release. Trout season won't open till May. Do you fish?" She wore jeans and a T-shirt with an obscure college name on the front, as I did. Cheap seconds from the outlet store.

I leaned over and stuck a hand in the frigid water. "No. Do you?"

"Nope. My ex did."

I sat on a rough handmade bench nearby. She joined me. "Peaceful, isn't it?"

Wasn't that what people claimed they were looking for when they flocked to the shores and beaches, threatening to overwhelm them with development? They planted lawns, then fertilized and mowed down to the water, destroying the natural habitat. They pulled out the native plants and clear-cut a treeless view of the water. In the end their vacation property resembled their city residences—groomed, unnatural, unable to sustain wildlife.

As if she read my mind, she said, "The DNR put in rocks to protect the shoreline. Otherwise, the property's just like I found it. Want to see the cabin?"

I followed her up the hill. Stale air met us when we stepped inside. Most of the interior was visible from where we stood. An enclosed porch with windows all around faced the trout stream. Beds were set up on either side with a table and chairs in the middle. Behind one side of the porch was a tiny kitchen with enough space for a small gas cooking stove, a few feet of counter space with cupboards over and under and drawers in between, a porcelain sink and drainer with storage space beneath, and an old rounded fridge. Next to the kitchen was a longer room with beds along the walls and shelves over them. A Franklin-type stove stood in one corner. The floors were wood with a few rag rugs thrown over them. Before we went out the small screened-in back porch to get the cooler, she pointed out the bathroom, which was just behind the kitchen. It held the toilet, a small sink, shower stall, and water heater and was the only room with a door.

"Nice place." I was thinking I'd be here on weekends if it were mine.

"Thanks. I bought this property with my ex-husband. It's a good investment, but it's kind of lonesome."

I stopped in my tracks and she nearly jerked the cooler out of my grip. We had a hand on either end.

"I didn't know you were married."

"Twelve years. That's when he got the itch. I thought I'd be glad when he left. I didn't think I'd miss him."

We set the cooler on the floor in front of the fridge, and she bent to unload it. "Hope you like burgers and beans. I wanted to keep it easy."

"I do." I studied her back as she emptied the cooler contents into the fridge. "You miss him?"

"I think I miss having someone to talk to. A presence. In the end he was never home anyway."

"Tell me about him."

"He's an attorney, too. Nelson Barrows. We met in law school. Mona knew him. She started working at the firm the year he left. He lives in Madison and is doing spectacularly well." She turned and gave me a grave smile. "He's the ambulance chaser."

I knew firsthand that rejection, even if you wanted to be rid of the person, was hard to swallow. "You haven't been with anyone since?" I had no idea where I stood, if I was just a friend or what.

She closed the fridge and faced me. "Not really. What about you?"

"The last person left after Mona moved in. About six years ago."

"Lisa?" she asked.

"Yes." My face flushed.

She smiled sweetly. "Mona told me years ago you were gay."

"Wish I'd known."

"Hey, it's okay."

"Why wouldn't it be?" I shot back.

She stammered, "What I meant is I don't care. I've always suspected I was a . . ."

"Lesbian?" I finished for her when she paused. "You don't know?"

"I thought maybe you could help me with that."

"You can't be my client and my friend," I said, when I should have been leading her to one of the beds.

"I don't want to be your client, but I do want to be your friend." She slipped past me and threw open the windows on the porch. "It's a lovely day. We should be out enjoying it."

XIV

The sun brought out the smell of the pines. We walked down to the stream again and followed a path along its banks. Rivulets of water drained through the wetlands between the shoreline and the hill and entered the creek. I looked through the dark water to the golden sandy bed beneath.

"Did your husband catch fish here?"

"Brown and brook trout. Sometimes a sucker."

I'd ask Mona what she remembered about Nelson Barrows.

At Sally's property line we made our way uphill to the sandy road. We walked past a few houses to where the road ended in a cul-de-sac. The homes looked like permanent residences.

On the way back we passed Sally's two-track road, the cabin hidden from sight, and continued on to where the sand road turned into blacktop. Passing more houses on either side of the pavement, some of them very large and very old, we came to the road that ran through the village of White Pine. Across the street was the River Crossing, a barn of a bar.

We leaned on the railing over the dam that created the millpond adjacent to the River Crossing. The water fell thick and noisy below us, spraying our faces.

A truck sped into the parking lot, spitting sand. A large man climbed out of the cab and called, "Come on in, Sal. I'll buy you a drink."

"Want a Coke or a beer?" she asked me.

I hadn't had an alcoholic drink before noon since I'd graduated college, but I was thirsty. "Sure."

"That's Ted Kersey. He owns the place."

We walked into a cavernous room with a bar along one side, tables on the floor, a corner for dancing in front of a stage. The windows were all along the porch and river sides, where the sunlight struggled to get through the dirt.

Ted stood inside the door, his arms spread wide. "Where have you been, and who's your friend here?" He was a tall man and big, heavy. Sally looked lost in his hug.

She introduced me and he shook my hand. "Nice to meet ya. Drinks are on me. What can I get ya?" He moved behind the bar.

What the hell, I thought. "A beer, draft. Please."

Sally asked for the same.

He placed some quarters on the counter. "Pick out some tunes."

Sally gestured for me to follow her. The jukebox selections were either pop or country. "Got any favorites?" she asked.

"Not really. Nothing too twangy."

We climbed onto the bar stools to Patsy Cline's rendition of "Crazy." The cold liquid slid down my throat. Sally and I thanked him.

"You should come in more often," Ted said.

"Maybe I will now that it's spring. How was the winter?"

"Dry. Cold. Quiet except weekends. The dancers come in then." He grinned and his eyes nearly disappeared in the bulging of his cheeks. He poured himself a beer and slugged it down. "Want some popcorn?"

"I'd love some," I said, and he plugged in the popcorn machine, poured oil in the popper, and added salt and popcorn.

"What's new?" Sally asked him.

"Well, my wife left me. Said I was too fat. We've got a library now, just down the road."

"I'm sorry," Sally said. "I don't think I ever met your wife."

Ted waved her words away. "She didn't come into the bar. Allergic to smoke. I don't have to worry about hurrying home now."

Sally said, "Still, it's never easy."

"Guess we both know what that's like." Ted shrugged off her sympathy. "I don't mind. I'm too old to change my ways. I nearly had to sell the place, though. She got half the goods."

"I know," Sally murmured, and I wondered if she'd had to buy out her ex-husband's share of the law firm and house.

We paid for the next beer and ate two bowls of popcorn before leaving. "Want to go see the new library?" Sally asked, as we stood in the hazy sunlight back on the road.

"If you do," I said.

"Another time maybe. Right now I'd like to go back to the cabin."

We strode along the road under the now warm sun and climbed the hill to the small cottage. Inside, Sally asked, "Hungry?"

"No." I wanted only one thing.

She turned and looked me full in the eye. I gathered my courage and took a step toward her. "What do you say we find out if you're a lesbian?"

She backed up against the table, her cheeks reddening, as I closed the distance between us. Leaning into her, I inhaled her breath, beery and warm. I heard her swift intake of air as I touched her lips with mine. Her mouth crumpled softly.

I wanted to sustain that first kiss, always so exciting and filled with promise, but I noticed her eyes slewing sideways toward the windows and doors. I released her. "Are you expecting someone?"

"No. It's just that everything is so open. Let's lower the blinds."

Feeling a stab of excitement, I hurried around with her to let the blinds down. She locked the doors. Then we stood in the middle of the room, looking at each other.

"Which is your bed?" I asked, when she seemed struck speechless.

She led me to one on the porch. All the beds were twins with a trundle bed underneath. In that small cabin there was as much sleeping space as I had at home.

We took our shoes off and climbed between the cool sheets. Pressing close, I felt as if I were sinking into her and rose up on an elbow so that I could look into her face. Her expression was unreadable.

"It's okay if you don't want to," I felt obliged to say.

"I'm just nervous, is all. I've never done this before."

I hadn't had a woman since Lisa, except for an occasional one-night stand. It was my feeling that sex came naturally to anyone who ever masturbated. I covered her body with mine, pushing her hair away from her face, its fine thickness entangled my fingers. I gently kissed her eyebrows, her eyes, her cheeks and neck and mouth, this time deeply.

"Clothes," I said, coming up for air. "Can we take them off?"

After thrashing about, I threw off the sheets and blankets and dropped my clothes on the floor. I helped her remove hers, then drew the covering over us. I was sweating with the effort, and she still wore her bra and panties.

Running a finger down her cleavage, I said, "Come on. No fair."

Then we were as one, skin against skin. I'd forgotten how the softness of a woman moved me, how her giving of herself for my pleasure made me grateful.

I pushed my thigh into the damp mat between her legs. I knew I was rushing things, but it had been so long. She arched backwards and I kissed her neck, until she grabbed my head and kissed me back.

Breaking away and moving down her body, I buried my head

94

between her breasts, thinking I would gladly asphyxiate there, drawing as my last breath the smell of her skin, the malleable breasts my pillows. But I moved on in my quest for orgasm.

Sally imitated my caresses, slowing when I did, speeding up to my rhythm. Our moans became a duet in the cottage. Outside blue jays screeched and sandhill cranes warbled from somewhere farther away. A skein of geese flew overhead, honking as they went. A persistent phoebe called from nearby.

When we lay back in the single bed, panting, I smiled and lifted myself up on my elbow. "Well?"

"Well what?" she asked, her chest and face flushed.

"Are you or aren't you?"

She gave me a shy smile. "I think I need to do that a few times to make sure."

I laughed and bent over to kiss her, smelling the sex on both of us. "We will, when I catch my breath. We'll do it differently." I thought of all the ways there were to make love.

"How?" she asked, molding herself into my side.

Putting an arm around her, I said, "I'll show you."

Later, when the sun slipped behind the trees, we got up and showered. The faucet sputtered and blew air out of the pipes before settling down to a steady stream. We squeezed into the small stall together. I lathered her and she me, then we rinsed and dried each other off.

Sex always released my tongue, much the way drink does for others. It also made me ravenous.

At dinner I spoke about growing up with Mona and Craig. How Craig was favored as the son, how, even then, Mona exhibited unusual energy. I even talked about my own inhibiting shyness. Hormones had set me on edge, probably because I didn't know how to direct them. My crushes had been on the cheerleaders, not the football players.

I'd brought a bottle of wine, and we were on our third glass when I asked, "Did you have crushes on girls?"

She smiled and shrugged. "I was too busy studying."

"You were valedictorian, weren't you?" I asked, remembering. She nodded. "I never went to the prom or any of the dances."

"Did that bother you?"

"Yes. Sure. I was one of the class nerds. Mona was my savior."

"Did you have a crush on her?" I hoped not.

"I don't know. Maybe. She saved me from social disgrace." She smiled again.

"You have such a nice smile."

"So do you."

We went outside to watch the sun set, which was hard to see through the trees. Sitting on lawn chairs, looking down at the stream, we finished off the wine. The warmth faded with the sun, and we bundled up in jackets till the chill of darkness sent us inside.

When we climbed into the single bed with books in hand, I was so distracted by her nearness that I read the same paragraph three times. Putting my book on the floor, I threw an arm around her and fell asleep, while she read on.

I awoke to the sound of the blue jays, the phoebe, the sandhill cranes. Sally slept, her behind tucked into me. I went to the john and climbed back in bed, amazed that I'd fallen asleep so easily the night before. Picking my book off the floor, I read till she stirred into wakefulness.

Thunder rumbled in the distance when we made love that morning. Even the most intimate moments failed to satisfy my need to be close to her.

When we left for home, we dashed through sheets of rain, threw our stuff in the backseat, and jumped inside. We drove through a waterfall on the steep hill down to the road.

"What's next?" she asked, when we were nearly home.

"You tell me," I said. "We can be as close or as distant as you want."

"What do you want?"

"To get away from Mona and Shirley."

"I'm your way out. Do you want to move in with me?"

"That's not what this is all about. We could spend some nights together, see how we like it." I'd been mulling this over most of the day. Do you just make love and go your own way or do you make love and immediately become a couple? Somewhere in between was more to my liking.

When she parked in my driveway behind Shirley's truck, I leaned across the seat to kiss her. "Sure you don't want to come in for a few minutes?" She had work waiting at home.

"Love to, but I can't. I leave you to Mona and Shirley." She gave me a wicked grin.

"Thanks. I'll be thinking about how I can repay you for that." I grabbed my bag and high-stepped it through the puddles to the house.

Shirley and Mona looked up from the kitchen table when I walked in, their fingers wrapped together. "Where's Sally?" Mona asked.

"She went home."

"We're having snacks. Want to join us?" Shirley asked.

Shirley's voice was deeper. I looked more closely at her. "You look different."

"I am," she said. "I'm reversing the process."

"What process?" I asked.

"Don't look at him that way," Mona snapped.

Him? "What way?"

"Like he's some weirdo. He's a man."

Shirley looked embarrassed.

"Can I talk to you a minute?" I asked Mona.

"Whatever you have to say you can say in front of Shawn."

So it was Shawn now. "Okay. What do you know about Sally's ex-husband?"

"Oh," she said. "Nelson? Good-looking jerk is what I recall."

"Why was he a jerk?" I set my bag down, sat at the table, and popped a cracker with cheese in my mouth.

"He was interested in his advancement. He left her cold when he was offered a partnership in a Madison firm. She was devastated and hard pressed to buy him out. Why?"

I shrugged.

"You're doing it, aren't you?" She jumped up and jabbed a finger at me, which I wanted to break off.

"Come on, Mona. That's not your business," Shirley/Shawn said.

"Mind your own business," Mona shot back at him.

I was now thinking of Shirley as a he. He needed a shave. I saw no trace of breasts under the flannel shirt he wore tucked into his jeans.

"What's to eat?" I got up and looked into the fridge.

"We're taking care of dinner," Shawn said.

"Great. I'll go unpack." Not that I had much stuff to put away, but I wanted to defuse Mona. I grabbed my bag and walked through the dining and living rooms to the stairs. Even though it was raining out, the paint job and new carpet made the house lighter, brighter. In my room, I greeted the naked ladies with a grin.

XV

Sally called during dinner. "I miss you. Can you come over?"

"I thought you had work to do," I said, turning away from Mona.

"It's done. Why don't you stay the week?"

"I'll come later," I promised.

As soon as I hung up, work called. One of the newer staff was on call, wanting to know what to do with Anna, who had been picked up by the police after being reported missing by Providence House.

"She says she went out for a walk, is all."

"Tell them to take her back there. Maybe she did just go out for a walk."

"In this rain?"

"She's not always aware of things like hot and cold and rain. Did you call Tracy? She's Anna's caseworker."

"Couldn't reach her."

"I'll stop in and see Anna tonight. I'm going to be in town."

"Here, let me warm that up," Shawn said, putting my plate in the microwave, when I sat down to eat again.

"Thanks." I smiled.

"Mine's cold, too," Mona said, holding out her plate. "Are you going to Sally's tonight?"

"Yep. I don't know how long I'll be staying."

"Nance called, looking for you."

"Just to talk or what?"

"She doesn't confide in me," Mona said.

"Is something the matter?" I asked, knowing it was better to get whatever was bothering her out where I could deal with it.

"You go flouncing off for the weekend, come back to a ready-made meal, and then take off again for God knows how long. We're not the caretakers here."

"You live here, don't you? For free?" I'd hardly gone anywhere in years. "You were the one who went to visit Mom and Dad."

Shawn set our warmed food in front of us. He reached for Mona's hand. She shook him off and rose to her feet. "You won't even let me update the house where I have to live." Throwing down her napkin, she stalked from the room.

"I should go after her," Shawn said.

"If you want to be verbally abused, go ahead." My appetite was gone. "I think I'll leave now." I felt badly for him. "Mona's a volatile person."

Mona was sitting on the couch, arms crossed. "Going to pack?"

"Why do you care? You have Shawn."

She tossed her hair, and I pictured her as a girl, angry at the world. "I don't care. Tell Sally hello."

She'd gotten what she wanted, and Shirley, who was now Shawn, was not exciting enough. Typical. And what had Shawn gotten? Not his sex change operation. But she was my sister. I loved her. "I will."

I called Nance from my bedroom. "What's happening?"

"I was going to invite you over to dinner last night. I'd ask you to come tonight, but we already ate."

"So did I."

"Where'd you go yesterday?"

"Mona didn't say?"

"I got Shawn on the phone. Apparently, he's moved in."

"Oh yes. I guess he's decided to remain a he. Mona can be very persuasive."

"Dennis said he looked and sounded as if he'd changed his mind. Come on, tell me where you were and with whom? I hope it's not someplace boring, like a conference."

"I was at Sally Shields's cabin. Lovely place."

"So, you and Sally are an item? She's Mona's boss, right?"

"Right to the boss part. I'll be at her place tonight, maybe longer."

"You're not going to stay with us when you're in town anymore?"

"I didn't say that. What's new on your end?"

"Nada. Dennis says hello."

"Hello back. Got to pack my bags again."

"Okay. How about lunch Monday?"

"Tuesday's better." Mondays were filled with meetings.

The rain had slowed to a drizzle when I stopped at Providence House on the way to Sally's. Jane Dougherty unlocked the door for me. She was one of the younger staff members. "Hi, Abby. They just brought Anna back."

"Did she just wander off?"

"The front door was unlocked. She's in her room. She's not very happy. I'll take you there."

I knocked lightly on the partly open door. Anna was sitting on a bed, her hands loose in her lap. She wore lavender sweatpants and sweatshirt. Her hair glistened with raindrops.

"Hi, Anna. Can I come in?" I stepped into the room. There were clothes on the other bed. "How are you?" I asked.

"You again," she said accusingly. "You probably put me in here."

"I brought you something good." Chocolates. I hoped she might have a sweet tooth as so many of the elderly do.

She looked at the box suspiciously. "Poisoned probably."

"I'll eat one, if you like." I sat on one of the orange plastic chairs.

She narrowed her eyes as I opened the box and popped a caramel chocolate in my mouth. My favorites. I held the box out to her. She grabbed it and looked under the lid, then took a bite out of a pecan turtle. A panicky look crossed her face as she swallowed and sat still, apparently waiting for something terrible to happen.

"Can I have another?" I asked.

Clutching the box to her, she said, "Indian giver."

I nodded at the other bed. "Who's your roommate?"

"She's out to get me."

"What makes you think that?"

"She sneaks in here when she thinks I'm asleep and peers at me." The woman was probably afraid of her.

I stood up. "I can't stay long, but I'll come back soon to visit."

"When can I get my own place?"

"Tracy's looking." I didn't have much hope that she'd be able to live on her own anymore.

"Will you bring me some chocolates?"

"You bet." I smiled. For the moment, anyway, she didn't think I was trying to kill her. I took that as a compliment.

Parking in front of Sally's garage doors, I hurried through the misting rain to her front door.

She smiled. "Am I glad to see you."

"You just saw me a few hours ago." I set my bag on the floor of the foyer and went to get my hanging clothes. Back inside, I handed her the hangers and removed my jacket. The house was warm and smelled of bread.

"A few hours can be a long time."

"Tell me about it. I've just spent those hours with Mona and

Shirley, who is now Shawn, although he's a really nice person."
And Anna, although I didn't mention her name.

"Shawn?"

"He's stopped taking his hormone pills."

She took my hand and led me up the stairs to her room. I understood. We were starved. She, because she'd never had sex with a woman. Me, because it had been years since I'd had sex with anyone but myself.

It was as if we hadn't just come together that morning. We dropped our clothes on the floor as we made our way to the bed. At first I wanted nothing more than to melt into her warmth, her softness. But when we kissed, passion took over and we were off and running.

Afterwards, although it was only eight-thirty, I slid further under the covers, loath to get up again. Outside, branches bent in the wind, outlined in the light of a streetlamp. Rain slid down the windows.

"I have to run downstairs and turn out the lights," she said.

"I'll get my stuff."

She touched my arm, her pupils huge in the bedside lamp. "I'll do it."

I did have to get up, though, to use the bathroom. When I slid under the sheets once more, she was there. I ran fingers through her thick hair, kissed her mouth, then picked up my book. We read, sides touching as if we were still in a single bed.

At work Monday, my fellow crisis workers and I were in the tiny kitchen, filling up on coffee and Danish sweet rolls, when Sylvia crowded in with us.

"Can I talk to you for a minute, Abby?"

"Sure." I followed her to her office and she closed the door behind us.

"You've heard me talk about my daughter, Linda, who was accepted at Northwestern and wanted to join the military."

"I thought she changed her mind and went to the university extension."

"She did." She heaved a sigh. "She told me she's a lesbian."

"Oh," I said noncommittally, "and how do you feel about that?"

Irritation crossed her face. "This is me, Abby. I'm not a client. I'm okay with it. It's her dad that's the problem."

"Sorry. What did he say?"

"It's not what he said, it's the way he interacts with her. Like she's someone else's kid." She fiddled with the stapler on her desk. "Can I ask you what your parents said or did when they found out about you?"

"Sure. We didn't talk about it, even though it was the elephant in the room, and then they moved to Arizona." Dad always chose to ignore family things he couldn't control or change. Although my mother was disappointed in the beginning, probably because I wouldn't be giving her grandchildren, she never asked questions. They liked Lisa, but they treated her as one of my friends, not my partner, not like Mona's husband or Craig's wife. We don't want to think of our parents as sexual people, and they probably don't care to think of their children that way either. "Give him time to get used to the idea."

Before beginning our morning staff meeting, Debbie asked, "What did Sylvia have to say?"

"Personal stuff." I dumped my purse on the floor and sat on a chair facing the couch where they were lined up with Debbie in the middle.

"She always talks to you," Debbie said, a little wistfully.

"That's not true." It wasn't, of course. Sylvia had thought I could give her some insight into how to handle a lesbian in the family, which made me want to laugh. All these years and I still wasn't comfortable enough to discuss my sexuality with anyone other than my closest friends. Had I mentioned Sally to my mother? Of course not.

XVI

Nance and I sat at what I considered Sally's and my table. The waiter strutted over with coffee and water. I nodded and smiled.

"Got yourself another girlfriend," he remarked.

"You're cheeky," I replied.

"No, I'm Alexander." He poured the water. "Coffee?"

"Decaf," we replied together.

Nance laughed when he sashayed off. "Why are gay men funnier than straight men?"

"Don't lump us together."

"You're not a gay man. Lesbians don't fit in the funny category. They take life seriously."

"There you go again, generalizing," I said, but I wasn't annoyed. I didn't actually care. I sipped my coffee and wondered how Mona and Shawn were making out, an unfortunate choice of words.

"Tell me about this new woman. Name, profession, age, weight, height. Actually, a picture would be best. Do you know how long it's been since you dated a woman?"

"You know Sally Shields. She was Mona's best friend in high school."

"Sally Shields," she repeated, raising her voice alarmingly. "I'd forgotten. I didn't know she was a—"

I put a finger to my lips. "Don't tell the world. Okay?"

"I was going to say *attorney*. Does she do divorces?"

"What? You're not divorcing Dennis. You'd be crazy to even think about it."

"If you think he's so great, why don't you live with him?" She took a sip of coffee and we ordered.

Alexander went off saying, "Soup and bread, soup and bread," as if it were hard to remember.

"I met someone the other day who's selling his house. He's gorgeous and he's funny and he likes me."

"Maybe he's gay," I said. "You just said—"

"I know what I said. He's not gay." She leaned forward over the table and hissed, "He ravished me on his tan leather couch when I went to measure his house."

The correct word for what I felt would be *aghast*. So taken back that I momentarily lost my breath, I stammered, "What about Dennis?"

"Hasn't something like that ever happened to you? One minute I was on my feet and the next I was on the couch." She gave me a trembling smile and started to cry. Tears rolled down her cheeks, smearing her mascara. She dabbed at them with the napkin, smudging the makeup further. "Don't tell Dennis."

I promised I wouldn't. If she didn't want Dennis to know, she wasn't serious about divorcing him. Why would I want to bear bad news anyway? "Is this a one-time thing?"

"I'm meeting him at the house again tonight to sign the paperwork." Her eyes swam, bright and excited.

"Can't you do that in your office?"

The food appeared in front of us, and we thanked Alexander,

who shuffled around for a moment as if he had something to say. He did. "Is that other woman you're usually with an attorney?"

"Yes. Why?" I asked. He was good-looking in a fine-featured, girlish sort of way.

"Does she do contracts?"

"Yes. I have her business card." I gave it to him and he went away, studying it.

"I want one, too," Nance said, holding her hand out.

When we were alone, I gave her some advice. "Don't sleep with two people at once. It's confusing. You live with Dennis, so you see the good and the bad in him all the time. You only see what the other person wants you to see. He has an unfair advantage."

"There's another way of looking at that. Dennis and I own property together. I'd lose my shirt if I left and so would he. I don't want a divorce attorney. I just briefly lost my head."

Leaning forward, I hissed, "Think about all the STDs out there."

"The what?" she asked, looking amused.

"The sexually transmitted diseases."

She raised her brows. "Oh, those. He looked so clean."

"That doesn't mean a thing," I said.

"I could say the same to you. Maybe you need a dental dam. Now tell me all about your involvement with Sally."

I told her what there was to tell, which seemed surprisingly little compared to how it felt. I thought I could be really happy with Sally, but I said, "It'll never work, because when Shawn leaves Mona, I'll have to pick her up off the floor."

"You're such a martyr," Nance said.

"I am not," I protested.

"Yes, you are. Mona can live alone. Just keep an eye on her."

I sighed.

Our lunch ended in laughter over something I immediately forgot. We could never stay serious for long when we were together.

❧

107

I called Mona at four in the afternoon. She was usually home by then. She picked up on the third ring. " 'Lo. Mona speaking." I heard noise in the background. A radio? A TV?

"It's me, Mona. How are you?"

"Shawn and I are planning a party next Saturday to announce our marriage. You're the first to be invited."

"You got married?" I asked, alarmed.

"Not yet." She giggled. "Next month. You'll be my maid of honor, but I don't know how honorable you are." She hooted a laugh.

For the second time that day, I was stunned. "Isn't it kind of soon? What about the sex change?" What had happened to Shirley?

"I told you, Shawn's changed his mind—at least for now. If he does it, it'll be after the marriage. I'll need your help with the house, the food, the usual stuff."

"Of course," I said, my mind racing forward. "I won't be home tonight, but I have to come over tomorrow to pick up more clothes. We can talk then."

On the way to Sally's I stopped in at Providence House. Anna was sitting on her bed, dressed in the same clothes, as if she'd never moved.

"Don't you want to meet the other people here?" I asked.

She scowled at me. "Did you bring me something?"

I hadn't. "You ate the entire box of chocolates already?"

"None of your beeswax," she snapped and asked suspiciously, "What are you doing here anyway?"

"You're on the way to where I'm going." The other bed was made up and I saw no possessions on or near it. "Where's your roommate?"

"Gone. I want to go home, too," she said plaintively.

There was no home, of course. She couldn't go back to her

daughter's place, her apartment was rented to someone else, and Tracy hadn't found a room for her. "I know," I said soothingly.

"You don't know nothing," she barked back.

The afternoon was warm, the air sweet-smelling. The windows were thrown open on the river side. Gulls screeched overhead and a flock of geese honked as they skidded to a landing in the water. Sally sat on the porch, reading the paper.

"I've got a news flash," I said, and told her about Mona and Shawn's planned marriage.

Sally stared at me. "She didn't tell me, but then I was in court most of the day."

"I'm supposed to be maid of honor." I saw myself dressed in a satiny gown, as I had been the first time Mona married, heading down the aisle. "I think I'll suggest they do this in the courthouse."

"Should they be doing it at all? They just met." She looked stunned.

"I'm going home tomorrow. I'll probably stay overnight. I don't know when I'll be back."

"I'll miss you." She smiled. "Are you hungry?"

"Always," I said, but I wasn't referring to food.

At ten the next morning I ushered Elizabeth Halbertson into my office. She perched on the edge of the chair, clutching her purse as she had before. Ready to run.

"You're safe here, Elizabeth."

"I'm not safe anywhere." Her voice trembled. "Jim's parents are raising the money for the bond. He'll be out."

I sensed her fear, a tangible thing. The folly of parents who took their kids' sides no matter what their children did was well known here. Kids who used their parents as shields against the law thought they were entitled to special treatment. In the end, unless they were wealthy, they found out differently. In this case, it occurred to me that the parents might be afraid of their son.

I phoned Sally and dropped the question in her lap. "Is it true that James Brume is going to be released on bond?"

"His parents have come up with the money."

"Why didn't you tell me this last night?" I asked angrily.

"I didn't know last night."

"How soon?"

"His hearing is scheduled for this afternoon. Look, Abby, I shouldn't be discussing this with you."

"Then don't." I hung up, steaming. I'd counted on Sally to keep me informed on Brume's status, but why would she? I cooled down a little, knowing I should have made my own inquiries.

"Hang in there," I said to Elizabeth and phoned the women's shelter. There was no room. The empty bed in Anna's room came to mind. The halfway houses were for our mentally ill clients, but maybe I could stretch the rules. "One more call."

Jane answered.

"This is Abby Dean, Jane. I need a bed. I was thinking about the one in Anna's room. Is it still available?"

"Actually, it is." I laid the facts out for her, because this might land us both in trouble.

"Send her over. I'll tell Anna she's got a new roommate. By the way, she gave me a chocolate."

"She must like you. Thanks for the bed."

I turned to Elizabeth. "Come on. Let's go pack a bag." Making arrangements and pointing Elizabeth in the right direction was okay, but to personally take part in her move might be frowned on by those higher up. At the moment, I didn't care. I'd told her I'd keep her safe. I picked up the phone and called the scheduling desk. "Cancel my morning appointments, will you? Something has come up. I'll be back by noon for sure."

We took the backstairs to the parking lot. Elizabeth stuck tight to me, frightening me with her fear, so that we both scanned the parking area as if expecting Brume to pop up from behind a vehicle.

"What about my car?" she asked as we crossed the lot.

"Take it. You can leave it behind the building. I'll follow you to your apartment."

She lived in the upstairs flat where Brume had held her hostage. "This place gives me the creeps, but every place I've looked you have to have a security deposit and a month's rent to move. I don't have that kind of money right now." She was stuffing clothes and personal items into a suitcase, which I lugged down to her car.

"What about work?" I asked before we drove to Providence House.

"I guess I'll have to quit. Who pays for the food at these places?"

"The county."

I went through the back door with her after Jane unlocked it. We took her bag to Anna's room.

"You," Anna said to me, giving me a narrow-eyed, thin-lipped look of disapproval.

"I brought you a roommate, Anna. This is Elizabeth."

"I don't want a roommate. I want my own room."

"We're looking, Anna. Elizabeth needs a safe place. I thought maybe you could give her that." Elizabeth stood next to me, shifting from foot to foot as if ready to flee.

Anna looked down at her hands. "Go away," she mumbled, "and take her with you."

"She has no place else to go."

"Shhh," Anna snapped and I knew she was hearing voices. "Okay. For a while." She raised her face. It was troubled. "They tell me wrong sometimes."

Lots of times, I thought. "Thanks. I'll be back tomorrow with chocolates." I turned to Elizabeth before leaving. "Walk me out."

Once we were out of earshot, I told Elizabeth about voices, how they sometimes direct people's lives. Mentioning names would have been a breach of confidentiality, but I thought Elizabeth would be able to put two and two together.

Elizabeth appeared startled as if she'd avoided a major catastrophe only to fall into something she understood less.

"The voices are in a person's head, but to that person they're very real. It'll be okay," I said, smiling and putting a hand on her shoulder. I could only hope.

"Thanks. I guess." She locked the door behind me.

XVII

After work, I braced myself to face Mona and Shawn's plans to wed. I vowed not to walk down the aisle of any church dressed in a sappy, too-young-for-me gown.

New corn, a few inches out of the ground, glimmered a bright green in the fields under a late May sun. The days were long and warm and redolent with growth. I drove with the windows open, sniffing at fresh-cut grass, which made me realize how much I missed the drive out to the house.

Bouncing down the gravel driveway, I parked next to Shawn's truck, a bright yellow four-wheel-drive F-250 with jazzy red stripes on the sides. It reeked of testosterone. Odd for him.

I walked through puddles of sunshine toward the back door, noticing how well everything had been trimmed. The garden was planted with vegetables and bordered with flowers. Unlocking the door and letting myself into the mud room, I heard raised voices and followed them through the kitchen and dining room to the living room.

"All I said was—" Shawn protested, covering himself with his arms, while Mona threw stuff at him—candles, coasters, magazines. She was getting into our mother's paperweight collection when I rushed to stop her.

"Stay out of this," she yelled, but I wrestled the key from her grasp and leaned against the hutch.

"You stay out of these. They're not baseballs. Mom would be furious."

"Sorry," Shawn said, dropping his hands to his sides.

"Don't you dare be sorry," Mona ranted, grabbing a book.

"Stop it," I said, taking hold of her throwing arm. "What's going on?"

"He doesn't want to invite people to the wedding. He's ashamed of me." Mona burst into tears.

"Hey," Shawn said softly, taking a step toward Mona, who backed away. "I'm proud of you. I'd just like a smaller wedding. We don't need a lot of people."

"I want my friends and relatives to be there," Mona sobbed.

I almost asked what friends and relatives she was referring to. All of our relatives, including our parents and brother, lived far away. If Mona had many friends left, I hadn't seen them in a long time.

"How about using the courthouse? A judge would marry you with only a few witnesses. Then we could have some people over afterwards." I looked from one to the other. "Have you made a list of who you want to invite?"

"He doesn't want to get married," Mona said sulkily.

I looked at Shawn for an answer. Would he have the nerve to walk away from Mona? He was beautiful, his wavy blondish hair cropped long, his eyes soulful. If he weren't so tall and broad shouldered, he could easily pass for a woman. His nostrils flared a little in the dust motes Mona had stirred up. She knew how to throw a ball. In high school she'd played on the girls' fast-pitch softball team. My dad had told me with pride that she could throw a ball sixty miles an hour.

114

"Let's sit down here at the dining room table," I suggested.

Shawn sat on one side of me, Mona on the other.

"Have you got a list?" I asked.

Mona withdrew one from her purse and unfolded it on the table. The mahogany wood shone in the overhead light; the walls gleamed. I scanned the names, seeing a few I knew and many more I didn't.

"How about we shorten the list to those who live here, ones you've had contact with regularly, Mona? Shawn will have his own list."

Besides people in her office and old high school and college chums, Mona's list included parents of old friends and aunts and uncles and cousins who had spread across the country. "Maybe you should talk to Mom about inviting these people."

"I like Abby's idea of getting married in the judge's chambers," Shawn put in.

Hoping Mona wouldn't think we were conspiring against her, I said, "It would save money, and after the ceremony, we could have an open house here." I turned to my sister, who was frowning.

"I've got a wedding dress picked out."

"You can wear it. Have you talked to Mom and Dad?"

She averted her gaze. "Yes."

"Are they coming?" I persisted.

"Yes. Of course."

"When is this planned?"

"June fifteenth."

"Are you ready for this? You've only known each other a few weeks."

"You moved in with Sally," Mona pointed out.

"I have not, and I'm not making a legal commitment with her." I glanced at Shawn, who, head down, was finger-combing his hair nervously,

"Maybe we should consider a fall wedding," he suggested.

"We agreed to summer." Mona's voice rose sharply. Fury took over, and she reached for a plastic fruit in the bowl on the table.

I grabbed the fruit before she could throw it. "This isn't something you force someone to do, Mona." I turned to Shawn. "What about the sex change operation—have you decided not to do that?"

Shawn nodded gloomily. "We have to get married while I'm still a man or it won't count. Besides we're going to have kids first."

"Kids first?" I repeated, disbelievingly.

He nodded.

"Are you sure you want to be a mother, Mona?" I said. She was not only terribly impatient, she was nearing forty.

"Yes, I do."

Today she did. Tomorrow, she might not. "Do you want me to set up a date in the courthouse with a judge? A Friday afternoon maybe. Then we can celebrate that night and have a breakfast the next day. Does that sound okay?"

"Who's going to get the house ready?"

"We will. The week before. we'll clean. You and Shawn can take care of the flowers and the caterer. I'll find a judge. The two of you better send out invitations for the reception this week. We need to know how many are coming."

Mona said accusingly, "You always take over."

"You're doing most of the work," I pointed out, getting up and pushing the chair in.

We ate in the kitchen. I'd bought a couple of pounds of hamburger, which Shawn made into patties, while I cut up potatoes for baked french fries, and Mona fixed a salad.

Shawn talked about the house he was helping Dennis build for A Home of Your Own. A low income couple with three kids had applied. It would be their first home.

"They're excited," he said, sitting down to dinner after grilling the burgers. "Nice family. Dennis offered the father a job. He's a roofer."

At least something was working out for someone, I thought.

Then Mona said, "James Brume was released on bond this afternoon. His parents remortgaged their house. Sally was furious. I heard her arguing with Don in his office."

"Isn't the girlfriend in danger?" Shawn asked.

"You bet she is," I said grimly. Anger made my voice unsteady.

"That's what Sally said to Don," Mona added. "What's Brume's girlfriend's name again?"

"Ex-girlfriend. Elizabeth Halbertson." I pictured her nervously clutching her purse and felt a chill of fear.

"I hope she's in a safe place," Mona said, looking at me, knowing I could probably answer that question but wouldn't.

After dinner, Shawn and I went for a walk in the sweet-smelling evening. Sunlight lay over the landscape, warm and mellow and pastoral in the dying day.

"I want you to know that I love Mona, that I'll take good care of her. If we have children, I'll be a good father." He strode alongside me, his hair shining in the light.

I glanced at him. "Have you considered the repercussions of a sex change operation? How it might affect your relationships with Mona and any kids you might have?"

"I would have it done when the kids were young, so it would seem as if it had always been that way."

"I'm afraid you're fooling yourselves. Mona is thirty-eight. She has bipolar disorder, and you want a sex change. And now you're talking about marriage and a family?" My voice rose a little.

"Is that so crazy? We don't have to have kids. I thought one kid might be nice."

"Kids are as unpredictable as Mona." A slight breeze whispered through the leaves. The warm sun lay like a blanket on my head and shoulders and caused me to squint.

"What should we do then? Not marry? Not have children?" He sounded despairing.

"I think you should wait. You hardly know each other."

"Tell that to Mona."

"That's another point. You can't tell Mona much of anything. Is that how you want to live?"

"It's like we're on a roller coaster and can't get off, you know? She says she can't live without me."

117

"She can," I told him, although I worried whether she'd want to or not. Why was I railing against their marrying? Mona had been married before. It had lasted fourteen years. This wasn't my business, I told myself. Let it go. "Who am I to say it won't work out?"

"Serious?" he asked with what sounded like relief.

"Serious."

"Are you going to stay with us for a while?" We had reached the end of the road where it T'd into a crossroad.

"We'll see." I was almost afraid to go to Sally's with Brume on the loose. I might say something I'd regret.

XVIII

I'd slept in so many beds in the past few days that when I woke disoriented in the night, I had to place myself in the right environs before getting up. I went to the bathroom and was starting back to my room when I saw a light downstairs.

Mona was reading on the sofa. The overhead light made an aura of her reddish-brown hair. "Can't sleep?" I asked.

"Nope. How about you?"

"I had to pee and saw the light. Figured it was probably you." I wondered why she wasn't cleaning or doing something active. She'd never been much for sitting still long enough to read a book. "What are you reading?"

She showed me the cover, a book about bipolar disorder that I had on my shelves. She gave me an ironic smile. "I hate the way I am. I know I'm a rotten sister most of the time. I thought getting married again would be a new start."

My heart twisted in sympathy, yet I said, "Taking your meds is the best thing you can do to retain normality."

A flash of irritation crossed her face. "I am. I know. I won't let Shawn down."

"You were throwing stuff at him a few hours ago," I pointed out.

"You're lucky I'm not throwing stuff at you right now. I was angry. He talked like he wanted out."

"If he does, it's better to decide now rather than after the vows have been said." It only seemed like we were having a normal conversation. It could dissolve any minute when or if Mona decided she'd had enough.

"It'll be all right. You'll see. Douglas and I lasted fourteen years."

"Douglas didn't want to be a woman."

Mona's hand tightened on the book. Her eyes glimmered, and I was sorry I'd put a glitch in her thinking. I sat next to her to tell her so, but she hit me with my book, then pummeled me with her fists.

"Hey, hey, hey," I said, grabbing her wrists. "I'm just being the devil's advocate."

"Let me go," she warned.

I did, as soon as it was safe, as soon as the strength went out of her arms, I gave her a quick hug and went up to bed.

At work the next day, I checked with Providence House. Anna and Elizabeth were getting along fine. The phone rang after I hung up, but I had to staff with the crisis unit. I let voice mail pick it up.

Karl Jankowski had come up on call the previous night. I dropped into a chair in the phone room, disappointed but not surprised. Karl hadn't turned up in ER in a while. "I think we should take him off the client list. I don't want to waste any more time on him. He's never going to change."

"I'm with you," Debbie said.

"I see no reason to continue a policy that hasn't worked," Bob agreed. "Maybe if we let him alone, he'll change his ways."

"Maybe he won't," Mark said. "Maybe he'll just drink himself to death."

"That's what he's doing right now, with or without our help," I pointed out.

"I'll take him on for a while, if that's okay."

"Maybe he needs a man's touch," I said, glad to be rid of Karl.

"I put Elizabeth Halbertson in Providence House for safety purposes. The women's shelter was full. If you remember, she's James Brume's ex-girlfriend, the one he held hostage. He's out on bail.

"Her problems date back to her childhood, to a controlling father, much like Brume. She learned her own worthlessness at his knee. I have to find some way to raise her self-esteem. Any ideas?"

They offered lots of insight into clients of their own with similar problems, but we all knew that one of the hardest things to do was to change someone like Halbertson's opinion of herself.

I listened to my voice mail when I returned to my office. Sally had called, asking me to phone her. I had a meeting in fifteen minutes.

"Hi, what's up?" I asked, my tone curt.

"Hey, it wasn't my doing," she replied softly.

"That doesn't matter, does it?"

"I told you, I can't take Don off the case, I can't even talk about the case. The judge set the bail. Please don't blame me for this. I'm as worried as you are."

"Yeah, well, you're not the one whose life is in danger."

"Will you come over tonight?"

"I can't, and I've got to go to a meeting right now."

"Okay. Bye."

I steeled myself against her voice. Its wistful, pleading note melted my anger and made me long to see her. I still felt she should have prevented Janssen from taking Brume's case, but the self-righteousness I'd wrapped myself in was rapidly dissolving.

The meeting was about disaster planning, not only for tornados and the like, but also about potential terrorist attacks. I was part of the trauma unit. It all seemed somewhat unreal to me.

After work, I bought a box of chocolates at Shopko and went to Providence House. The residents were just beginning to line up for dinner. I found Elizabeth and Anna in their room, and handed Anna the chocolates.

Elizabeth sought my eyes. "He's out, isn't he?"

I nodded. "I think so. Stay away from windows. Don't go outside."

"He might follow you here," she pointed out.

It was a possibility. "I won't come while he's on the loose."

"This is so hard," she said, her voice breaking.

"I know." But, of course, I didn't know. No one was after me. I could come and go as I pleased. "I'll call you."

Anna shuffled over and handed me a chocolate turtle before giving one to Elizabeth.

"Thanks." I popped it in my mouth and left.

Sometime that night James Brume showed up at Providence House. He may have followed me there. He may have seen Elizabeth's car in the parking lot. He wouldn't say later how he found Elizabeth.

I got the frantic call from Jane in the wee hours of the morning. "Elizabeth says James Brume is trying to get inside."

"Did you call the police?"

"Of course." Her voice rose to a hysterical pitch. "He broke a window. He's inside."

I hurried into my clothes and out the door into a warm drizzle. I knew I would get there too late to change anything. My job was to lessen trauma. The headlights focused on the black road, the wipers slapped back and forth, briefly clearing the windshield. I used the center line to navigate.

When I reached Providence House, two police cars with revolving blue and red lights were parked out front. I swung into the lot behind the building, parking near another squad car, and jumped out of the Saturn.

A policeman stopped me at the door. "You can't go in there."

"I'm Abby Dean from Crisis Intervention." I searched my purse for my ID badge and showed it to him.

The back hall was deserted. I headed toward the voices in the dining area, which rose in volume as I approached. Pausing in the doorway, I looked for Elizabeth. My heart pounded unnaturally loud. I saw Anna's white hair in the midst of a group of residents, Jane, and policemen.

She was saying, "Leave me alone. I want to go to my room," but no one seemed to be paying attention.

I made my way through the crowd to her side. She appeared befuddled. "Hi, Anna." Turning to the two policemen flanking her, one of whom was Scott McLane, I asked, "What's going on?"

He smiled thinly. "James Brume broke in and tried to take Elizabeth Halbertson hostage. Anna hit him over the head with a boot. Then everyone began hitting him. When we got here he was on the floor, out cold. He's back in jail where he belongs."

"He tried to kill Elizabeth," Anna muttered.

"Where is Elizabeth?" I asked.

"At the hospital. Her wound reopened. She'll be all right. The person on call went with her."

I took Anna to her room and talked to some of the residents. Jane was dealing with the others, who wanted to rehash the evening. I supposed none of them felt safe.

I was pretty worked up when I left, not ready to drive through the dark, wet night at two in the morning only to get up at six. Instead, I went to Sally's, where lights leaked through the blinds.

"I heard," she said, opening the door. "Don called. I phoned you, and Shawn said you'd been called out."

"Anna's an unlikely heroine in all this, but you don't know Anna." I'd phoned the hospital and been told Elizabeth was heavily sedated. I'd see her in the morning.

"Don's sorry he took the case. This guy, Brume, is scary. He cares only about getting even and insists that everyone else is at fault."

"Always the victim."

"Will you stay the night?"

"I don't have anything to wear tomorrow. I have to go home."

"You can wear something of mine," she said. "Come to bed and tell me about Anna."

I couldn't really tell her much about Anna, because most of it was confidential, but I went to bed with her and slept soundly till the alarm startled me into consciousness.

That morning I drove to the hospital after the staff meeting. Elizabeth was sitting up in bed, her arm again in a sling. She looked terribly pale and anxious. I pulled a chair up to the bed.

"I'm getting out today," she said. "I can't afford to be in here. No insurance."

I nodded sympathetically. Her entire existence had been put in jeopardy by Brume. She'd lost her job, her insurance, her apartment.

"You can stay in Providence House until you get back on your feet," I told her. I'd talked this over with Sylvia.

"How's Anna?" She gave me a wan smile.

"I haven't seen her today. Last night she just wanted to go to her room. She didn't seem to realize that she was the heroine of the day. The residents were all hyped up."

"They saved me. Anna saved me." Tears rolled down her face.

I handed her a tissue. Anna was more afraid of her voices than of someone like Brume.

"Things will work out, Elizabeth," I said without any real certitude. I'd do my best to help her take her life back. Exhaustion flowed through my limbs.

She took a few sobbing breaths and said, "How will I get to Providence House?"

"I'll take you."

After dropping Elizabeth off, I ate a bagged lunch and drank coffee, hoping to revive myself. The afternoon crept by. I found myself clock-watching, something I seldom did, and left promptly at five.

XIX

Mona, who'd recently taken up knitting to keep her hands busy, was working on a sweater for Shawn. She sat on the sofa, dropping the occasional loop and going right on. The needles clicked rhythmically.

"You didn't come home last night," she said flatly. "You should have called."

"And woken you up again? What did Sally tell you?"

"James Brume broke into the place where his ex-girlfriend was staying. He got knocked over the head by her roommate and beaten up. That's what she told me. It sounds unreal."

"It's real enough. He's back in jail."

"The girlfriend all right?"

"She's okay. Sorry the call woke you."

"It woke Shawn up, but he went right back to sleep. I was already awake. Want to play a game of cribbage?"

We hadn't played cribbage since Shawn moved in. "Sure," I said.

"I'm still thinking about adding a sunporch," she said, dealing out the cards.

"Let's do it." I picked up my hand. We had no mortgage payments. Why not make some improvements? If it made Mona happy, why not? From my perspective right now, life looked short.

"You mean it?" she said excitedly.

"I mean it." I put two cards in her crib.

She began to expound on the assets of having a sunporch.

"Play," I said. "We can talk about that later."

"You're going to be home tonight?"

"Yes."

"You're not going to Sally's."

"Nope. Over the weekend maybe."

"Why doesn't she come here anymore?"

"I guess because I haven't invited her."

"Well, ask her."

Shawn and Mona sent their invitations out on Saturday, driving into the city to the post office. I watched them go with their bag full of mail, feeling fatalistic, as if this were a turning point in our three lives. I hadn't decided whether I would move out when they tied the knot.

"You can't leave now that we're adding the sunporch," Mona said when she caught me perusing the classifieds. The design was one of Sun Sensations, but only the hot tub was theirs. Longworth Construction, Dennis's company, was doing the actual building. He'd promised to have it completed before the wedding.

Sally was coming over later in the day and staying overnight. I'd made a mushroom soup, prepared a bean dip, and started bread. Dinner would be pork roast with potatoes and carrots. Very basic.

I pulled on a sweatshirt and went for a walk. The sun burned through thin clouds, quickly heating me up, and I jerked the sweatshirt off and tied it around my waist. Red-winged blackbirds called from the tops of fence posts. They were weaving the tops of the taller grasses together for nests.

A sort of peace had fallen over me when I'd given up trying to change what now seemed inevitable. Mona and Shawn would marry and live in the house, maybe have kids. If Shawn wanted to be Shirley again, he would do so without any commentary from me. I'd let go of all that, or so I thought.

When the white rabbit ran into me in panic, I thought I must be seeing things. White rabbits don't live in the wild. I bent over and picked up its shivering body, protecting it from whatever had been stalking it. Thinking maybe it belonged to John, who was out in the field on his John Deere tractor, spraying the corn, put it in my car and drove to his house.

I walked through the barn, taking deep breaths of the dusty hay and sweet grain. Cats wound around my legs. John's son, Johnny, waved from the pasture beyond, where he was filling a water tank. I saw no rabbit hutches. Two dogs ran toward me, barking. I stood my ground and gave them each a pat.

I found John's wife kneeling in the newly planted vegetable garden behind the white two-story house. She smiled at my approach and got to her feet, wiping the dirt off her jeans. "Abby, how are you?"

"Fine. And you?"

"Who wouldn't be okay on a day like this. John's out in the field."

I seldom showed up at their doorstep. "I saw him. I found a white rabbit alongside the road. I wondered if it was yours."

She laughed. "We have a lot of animals but no bunnies. Somebody probably got it for Easter and dumped it. John's always finding abandoned dogs and cats."

"What does he do with them?" I asked.

"Takes them to the humane association or gives them to neighbors. We have all we can feed." She straddled a row of sweet corn, her hand shading her eyes, and smiled at me.

127

"Do you know anyone who might want a rabbit?"

She walked to the Saturn with me and looked in at the rabbit, who crouched on the floor, a slight tremor afflicting its ears. "A New Zealand White. They're meat rabbits. Nelsons, down the road, raise them for slaughter. They'd probably take it."

Maybe it was the trembling ears, but I couldn't bring myself to give the rabbit over for meat. "If I kept it, what would I need?"

"You could keep it in the house. It might use a litter box. They sell feed at the mill or at Fleet Farm. They also sell hutches if you don't want it inside."

I took it home and shut it in my bedroom, spreading newspapers on the floor and putting down a bowl of water, then drove to Fleet Farm to buy bunny food, a kennel, and a litter box.

When I got back, Shawn was outside digging a foundation for the addition, while Mona wheeled away the dirt and dumped it near the garden. They looked at me curiously as I carried my purchases into the house.

When Craig, Mona, and I were kids we'd always had a dog. Our parents' last dog had gone to Arizona with them and died on the way. Neither they nor Mona and I had owned another dog. Craig had one, I heard, but I thought a dog needed people around during the day. Maybe rabbits were different.

I found the rabbit hiding under my bed and after a few minutes of trying to lure it out, I left the door open and went downstairs. Curling up on the sofa, I read the newspaper and started on the crossword puzzle.

I was startled to see the white rabbit crouched nearby, looking at me, its pink nose twitching in apprehension. I said, "I forgot all about you." I had. I leaned over to pick it up, but it hopped out of reach. "How'd you like something to eat?"

In the kitchen, I set down a bowl with bunny food and another with water. The litter box I put near the door to the mud room. The rabbit took long hesitant hops over to the food and began to crunch on it.

When Mona came through the door, the animal fled toward the dining room. "What was that?" she asked.

"A rabbit I found when I went for a walk. I think I'll keep it if you don't mind."

"Mind? I've always wanted a bunny. Remember how I always begged for one at Easter time?"

I didn't and said so.

We named it Hops, unimaginative but apropos. When it finally got it through its tiny brain that we weren't going to hurt it, Mona held it on her lap and stroked its trembling body into sleep.

"What a good Hops," Mona crooned. We'd put it in the litter box after it ate and, sure enough, it performed.

When Shawn came inside to get something, she showed him the bunny. "Isn't he a great addition to the family? We haven't had a pet since Mom and Dad took Scooter with them."

Shawn turned Hops over and proclaimed him to be a her. "See? No balls, no penis, a vagina."

Mona was carrying the half-grown rabbit around when Sally arrived. I heard Sally talking to Shawn out back before she knocked on the door.

"A rabbit," she said with surprise when she came through the door.

I told her how I'd found Hops, and Sally stroked her as she lay cradled in Mona's arms. Her little pink nose twitched as she sniffed at this new person.

"Her hair is so soft, but she feels a little bony."

"Put her down, Mona, so she can eat."

We listened as Hops crunched the bunny food between strong teeth. After she ate and drank, I put her in her litter box. When Mona and I sang her praises, Sally laughed.

Shawn put some lettuce leaves and a little piece of carrot in Hops's bowl when he came inside. Sally and I carried the appetizers to the living room and waited for Shawn and Mona to shower and join us. I'd fixed the two of us each a vodka and tonic. I was through being responsible for Mona.

"God, what an awful week," Sally said. "Do you want to go to the cabin for Memorial Day weekend?"

"Sure."

"I want to get away. We can take Hops."

"I doubt if I can pry her away from Mona. I think it was love at first sight. How can you fall in love with a rabbit?"

"You brought her home."

The object of our conversation was hunched under the coffee table, her ears and nose twitching. "I couldn't leave her in the ditch. Something must have been chasing her, because she ran right into me and let me pick her up."

Shawn and Mona came downstairs, their hair wet, and went to the kitchen. Mona returned with a Diet Coke and Shawn a beer. They pulled chairs up to the coffee table.

"If the weather holds and if I get through digging, we'll pour the foundation on Monday," Shawn said.

Hops moved out from under the coffee table and hunkered under an end table. Mona picked her up and set her on her lap, then let out a startled noise. "She peed on me."

That night, I watched the naked ladies move in the shadows created by the bedside lamp. We'd shut Hops in the kitchen, where it would be easier to clean up after her, if necessary.

"It's the wind in the branches that makes them look like they're moving," I said. "Do they bother you?"

"No. I wish they were on my bedroom walls."

"Really?" I turned on my side and rested my head on my hand, so that I could see her better. "Maybe Mona would . . ."

She shook her head. "No."

"I know." I wouldn't trust Mona either after the painting debacle.

We made love, then fell asleep with our bodies touching lengthwise—legs, hips, arms and shoulder—in intimate slumber. I wakened to the sound of doves cooing outside the window and the heat of Sally's breath on my cheek. When I was fully awake and Sally still slept, I eased myself out of bed. Pulling on my dad's old bathrobe, the same one I'd lent to Shawn and then appropriated for myself, I went downstairs.

The rabbit lay on the old dog cushion we'd put down for her. I filled her empty food bowl and made coffee. Waiting with arms crossed till the dripping ceased, I carried two cups up the stairs. The rabbit followed me as if she were on a leash.

Sally opened her eyes when the two of us came through the door. I set the coffee down on her bed stand and climbed onto the mussed sheets, cradling my cup in my hands. "Morning." I bent over to kiss her.

She stretched and sat up, reaching for the steaming cup. "Thanks."

The rabbit jumped onto the bed, startling us both. It crouched at the far end, nose twitching, ears moving, beady red eyes fixed on us. We laughed.

"I think she's lonely," I said.

"I thought rabbits were solitary animals." She took a sip. "Mmm. Nothing like that first cup of coffee."

"She might make a good pet. She doesn't have to go for walks."

"Neither do cats."

"But cats kill birds. You can't let them run loose."

"Are you going to let her run loose?"

"Only in the house. Do you think that would be terrible? Being confined to a house?"

"For me, it would, but I'm not a rabbit." She glanced at the clock. "It's only seven."

"I know. I wake up every morning at six fifteen."

"What do you want to do today?"

"Ask me what I want to do right now," I said.

She set our coffee cups on the bed table and pulled me down beside her. Our feet bunched up against the rabbit. "Is this what you want to do?" She kissed me. Her hand moved over me in a caress that ended between my legs.

When we came up for air, I said, "Yep."

XX

Sally and I left for her cabin after work on the Friday of Memorial Day weekend. I'd purchased waders, a rod, hooks and sinkers, a sharp fillet knife. I'd bought a fishing license with a trout sticker. I was ready to give trout fishing a try.

The rod poked through the gap between the front seats. In the back were the cooler and our bags. We stopped at the River Crossing to buy worms from Ted.

His voice boomed over the heads of the customers seated at the bar. "Hello, girls. The fish is good tonight."

We looked at each other and decided to try it. Climbing onto the stools, we inhaled the smell of beer and smoke along with fish and fries.

Ted said, "Sally here owns the land that butts up to yours, Jerry."

The man next to me swiveled on his stool and stuck out a hand. "Jerry Whitlock."

Sally introduced us and we shook. Whitlock's skin had soaked up all the sun and wind it could take and now was the consistency of leather.

We'd left Hops home with Mona, who had become very possessive. Our food had been in the cooler less than two hours. It would keep. We could stay for hours if we wanted to.

"Get these ladies another beer," Whitlock said. "Do you fish?"

"I'm going to give it a go," I said.

"The best times are sunrise and sunset," he advised.

"Mmm," I murmured noncommittally, knowing I wouldn't be up with the sun.

Someone put money in the jukebox and a polka filled the large room. The older people began to dance. I glanced at Sally, hoping not to encourage Whitlock, who was slapping the counter. I didn't want to polka. After a while, he went to a table where he sat with friends, and I felt relieved. We ate our deep-fried fish, the coleslaw, rye bread, and french fries and left with the worms.

"Keep 'em in the fridge," Ted advised. "They'll last for weeks."

Outside, daylight lingered. It wasn't warm, but at least it was clear. We drove down the bumpy road, raising a cloud of sandy dust, and climbed the two-lane drive to the cabin.

Although it was lost in shadows at the bottom of the hill, we heard the trout stream rushing by. The interior of the cabin was cooler than outside and smelled musty. We carried in our bags and unloaded the cooler. Sally switched on the lights, bringing an illusion of warmth to the place.

In bed that night, we lay side by side. She was absorbed in papers that I assumed had to do with work. I was reading *In Her Shoes* and laughing when someone pounded on the door.

"Who is it?" Sally jumped out of bed in one leap and pulled on her sweats.

I followed hastily, dragging sweatpants and shirt on backwards. I hoped whoever was out there hadn't been peeking in the windows, hadn't seen us in bed together.

When Sally opened the door, Whitlock fell inside and stood

swaying on the piece of carpet laid down to catch sand. "Wanted to see if you girls got home safely," he said, squinting into the overhead light Sally had turned on.

"As you can see, we did," Sally said.

"I brought some beer to share." He waved a six-pack of Point.

"Not thirsty," she assured him. "Abby has to get up early tomorrow. She needs her sleep."

"I do," I said, nodding fervently, even though I had no plan to rise early.

"Want me to wake you up?" He looked out from under his brows, his head slightly bent, his body swaying.

"No. Please don't," I said.

He gave a sloppy salute and backed out the door. Sally shut and locked it and switched off the light. After listening to him move away through the brush, she dropped all the blinds.

"It never pays to be too friendly," she said, climbing back in bed.

I settled in next to her. If there had been any thoughts of making love, they were gone now. We would wait till morning.

She was a late sleeper, though. At seven, when she still hadn't stirred, I dressed and took my new purchases down to the trout stream.

A streak of sun burnished the amber-colored water to gold. The creek curled around itself, undercutting the bank, speeding over rocks and limbs. I pulled on the stiff waders, tied the sinker and hook to my fishing line, and put a worm on the hook. Yuck. The poor thing nearly came apart in my hands, and I found myself wondering how it would feel to be hooked.

Carefully stepping into the water, using a root to keep my balance, I felt the icy strength of the moving water. It nearly knocked me off my feet. Wading awkwardly toward an open patch, I cast my line and let it float. Something tugged almost immediately and I gave a little jerk and began to reel. The line went slack. Pulling it in, I saw the worm was gone. I made my way back to the bank and threaded on another, then struggled to the middle of the creek, and cast.

I'd been standing quietly for a few moments when two beavers swam toward me. They muttered to each other, their heads and backs and tails barely above the water. I froze in place and they swam past as if I were part of the landscape.

The sandhill cranes were whooping it up somewhere not too far away. I heard them clearly. A great blue heron landed in a shallow spot and began fishing with one eye on me. When something struck my line, the heron took off with a squawk, and I reeled in a brook trout. Before I could free it from the hook, it jumped out of my hands.

I was near shore when I saw the four deer make their way down a trail to the stream. A splashing downstream brought their heads up and in a moment they took off, tails flagging. Everything wild fled at the sight of me. I was the one who didn't belong.

Hearing splashing downstream, I saw Jerry making his way in my direction. Ducking behind a huge weeping willow, I climbed onto the bank, shook off my waders, and made my way uphill, hiding behind any cover I could find.

Sally was still asleep. It was only eight-thirty although it seemed as if it must be much later. I locked the door, washed up in the small bathroom, undressed, and climbed in bed with her.

She stirred under my cool touch. "You're like a chunk of ice," she murmured.

I slid cool fingers between her legs and coaxed her into a heated response. She moaned in my throat. "Did you catch anything?"

"It got away. I'll tell you later." I rolled her against me, undressing her, dropping her nightshirt on the floor. I thought I'd never get enough of the feel of her warm, smooth skin. Wiggling closer, I pushed her legs apart with my knee.

Later, when she was frying bacon and eggs and potatoes, she said, "I thought we would have trout for breakfast."

I told her about the beavers, the heron, the sandhill cranes, the deer, the lost trout, and Whitlock. "I half expect him to show up wanting to share a trout with us."

"Maybe he's lonely."

"I want to be alone with you."

135

But he didn't show up then or the followng two days. I hated the thought of going home.

When I returned to work on Tuesday, Tracy had yet to find a room for Anna. She stopped in my office, knocking on the door-frame. "Anna's raising a stink."

I knew that. Elizabeth had returned to work at Shopko and was looking at apartments. "It's better for her to be in a crisis bed than a room, though."

"Elizabeth has offered to take Anna in when she gets a place. She needs the money."

Anna wasn't easy. I knew little about Elizabeth. It would be an experiment in living together. "What about Anna's daughter? She was going to look in on Anna. How does she feel about this?"

"Guilty, but she can't get along with her mother. Why not give someone else a chance?"

"I'll talk to Elizabeth. I don't know if it's a good idea for her. I doubt if she's had any experience with someone as ill as Anna."

I left work early after calling Providence House to make sure Elizabeth would be there. Anna gave me a suspicious look, but said little. Elizabeth and I went outside to talk.

"I know she gets very angry and screams at times, but mostly she only mutters to herself," she said when I reminded her of Anna's condition.

"She's not in control of her reality. She hears voices. At times she's paranoid and you'll probably be the object of her mistrust. We'll have the mental health techs monitor her meds. Are you sure you want to live with schizophrenia? You may end up thinking you're mad."

Elizabeth looked down. She was leaning against her car, an old, rusting Toyota. "She saved my life."

"It looked that way to you."

"It was that way."

"I know. What I meant was it wasn't intentional on her part, although she seems to like you as well as she likes anyone. I suppose you could give living together a try. There will always be a crisis bed for Anna if it doesn't work out." I fully expected their arrangement to last a few weeks.

I was tempted to go to Sally's when I left, but instead drove home. It was only two weeks to the wedding. There was so much to do that I spent nights awake, going over a mental list. We had started with the bedrooms, vacuuming cobwebs, hanging out bedding, dusting. Working our way downstairs, we cleaned away years of neglect.

The sunporch was now enclosed with only the interior to finish in cedar. Shawn was working on it. I stepped inside. Sunlight shone through the skylights. The glass patio doors were thrown open, so that air could circulate through the screens.

"They're putting in the hot tub tomorrow," Shawn said.

I looked around, wondering why I had opposed this addition. "Nice," I said. "Is Mona home?"

"Not yet," he spoke around the nails in his mouth.

I went inside. The bunny waited, crouched near the humming refrigerator. I picked her up and took her to my room where sunlight nearly made the naked ladies invisible.

Lying on the bed with the bunny beside me, I thought of Anna whose hair was as white as the rabbit's. Anna had exhibited symptoms of schizophrenia in her late twenties, which was when her life spun out of control. Her daughter said her childhood was filled with fear of her mother's inexplicable anger, her paranoia which drove away friends and family, including Anna's husband. The illness gave Anna a flat affect. While the anti-psychotic medications tempered her moods, they did not change the dullness that robbed her of character.

Elizabeth's own childhood had not been better. The family had lived in fear of her father's displeasure. Not that he physically abused them. He used silence and withdrawal as emotional controls. Elizabeth said they tiptoed anxiously around his moods.

I'd begun to drift when Mona opened the door. "There's that bunny," my sister crooned, snatching Hops off the bed.

"I was almost asleep," I said crankily.

She withdrew and shut the door, but after a few minutes, I got up and went downstairs. Mona was dancing and singing to a CD with the rabbit cradled in her arms. She paused in mid-circle when she saw me.

"Hops hates the vacuum cleaner."

"Then why didn't you leave her with me?"

"Here, take her." She thrust the rabbit at me.

"Just put her down. Let her hide if she wants," I said, annoyed.

"Well, aren't you crabby."

I changed the vacuum cleaner bag and turned it on. I was irritable. I wanted to be with Sally. I wanted to sit down and read the paper. Intead, every spare moment was spent getting ready for Mona and Shawn's wedding, a wedding I thought was a mistake.

XXI

A week before the wedding, Shawn exhibited signs of imminent wedding remorse. His normally good-natured demeanor turned grumpy. He became restless and often came home late, claiming he had work to finish.

The sunporch was completed, the hot tub ready to use, although we hadn't been in it. We'd put a small table out there with four matching chairs and had been taking our meals under the skylights with the glass doors thrown open. June bugs, moths, mosquitoes, and flies buzzed at the screens for admittance. It was like being outside without the pesky bugs. I loved it.

Mona was pacing the kitchen, the rabbit in her arms, when I walked in the house on Wednesday. "He doesn't want to get married," she wailed.

"Did he tell you that?" I asked, although I suspected it might be true.

"No. He's too cowardly." Her eyes were red from weeping.

He's too kind, I silently corrected her. "Well, you can't assume it's true if he hasn't said so."

Everything was ready. Mom and Dad were flying in Thursday evening. Craig and his wife were arriving Friday morning. Their kids were old enough to leave at home. Other than our immediate family all the guests were close enough to drive. We were having a reception at the house Friday night and a brunch on Saturday, both catered. Now that I was resigned to this marriage, I was actually looking forward to the partying.

We ate on the sunporch, or rather I ate. Mona was too distressed. I finally made her put the rabbit down. Apparently, she found clutching her softly furred body comforting.

When the sun set and Shawn still wasn't home and hadn't phoned, I called Dennis.

"He was still working when I left. Want me to run by and see if he's still there?"

"I'm afraid he's not going to show up for the wedding. I know I didn't want them to get married, but everything's on go now, and he's getting soggy feet."

"I'll go look and give you a call. Don't worry. He'll show up for the wedding, even if I have to drag him there."

"Thanks," I breathed.

Mona wasn't in the house. I looked in the garage, saw her car, and went outside. I found her striding toward the road and ran to catch up with her.

"Where are you going?"

She never broke step. "This is your fault. He knows you don't want us to get married."

I hurried along next to her. "That's not true. Dennis is out looking for Shawn. He said Shawn was still working when he left."

Just then headlights turned into the driveway, framing us in their brightness. Shawn's truck rocked toward us. Tears coursed down Mona's face. Her fists clenched and she raised her face to the blue-black sky. I turned and went back toward the house. I was sitting on the sunporch with the bunny in my lap pretending to read the paper, when they both got out of Shawn's truck.

Mona ran in the back door and slammed it behind her. Shawn trudged after her in weighted boots. He paused at the sunporch and shrugged his shoulders in a futile gesture. It was all I could do not to say "I told you so."

I heard Mona weeping in the night, even though I wore earplugs. I fell into a restless sleep from which she wakened me before dawn with a rap on my door.

"Can I come in?"

It felt like old times. I pushed myself to a sitting position and switched on the bed lamp.

She looked terrible—her eyes red and swollen. "Don't," she protested, and I turned it off.

"Hey, it's going to be okay. Didn't Douglas get nervous before you got married?"

Sobbing, she shook her head.

"You just don't remember." I concocted a story about Douglas confessing last-minute doubts, which only made her cry harder.

"He didn't love me either."

"I made that up," I said. "Go back to bed, snuggle up to him, remind him of why he wants to marry you. Stop crying, for chrissake." Now I was annoyed. "I need to sleep, too."

"He just hunkers down under the sheet and pretends he can't hear me."

"Well, maybe he doesn't know what to do. Go give him some reassurance." Of course, she didn't have any to give. Her emotions, raw and loud, had taken hold. "Pretend."

She went back to bed then and I glanced at the clock. The sky was beginning to lighten. It was four-thirty. A bird began a hesitant song. More joined in. Soon they'd all be tuning up. I had a long day ahead of me. Clients to see, Mom and Dad to pick up.

❧

141

Anna wouldn't open the door when I stopped at Elizabeth's apartment on a whim. "Who's there?" she asked.

"Abby Dean," I said.

"You can't come in," she shouted.

"I just stopped to say hello."

"Go say hello to someone else. I'm not going anywhere."

Elizabeth had an appointment at nine-thirty. Setting her purse on the floor, she smiled when I told her Anna wouldn't let me in. The change in body language told me more than any words could. She no longer clutched her purse but leaned back in the chair, the hunted look gone.

"She thinks you're going to put her in the hospital or send her back to Providence House."

"I know. I'll forever be on her blacklist. How's it going, living with Anna?"

"Okay. She watches TV. I read. It's peaceful."

"Someday you're going to want more than peace."

"Not yet, though. I never realized how I always went for someone like my dad. It was like I was still trying to please him, wasn't it?"

I nodded. "People are more comfortable with the familiar." She'd been misled into equating possessiveness with love.

"I'm scared I'll make the same mistake again. Besides, it's nice having someone need me. Anna needs me. She doesn't say so, though, or act that way."

I explained how schizophrenia leaves a person with little interest or energy for anything.

At the end of the hour, she said, "Come by when I'm home. I'll let you in."

"Maybe I will. Give a call if you have any problems."

When she left, a hint of lily of the valley cologne lingered. The receptionist buzzed to say that Karl was in the waiting room.

Karl had asked to see me, although he was officially Mark's client. He followed me down the hall to my office and sat in the chair Elizabeth had vacated. Cleaned up, he looked fragile. A little stooped, broken blood vessels on his cheeks and nose, his eyes rheumy, his sparse hair combed back wetly. His shirt and jeans hung loosely on his thin frame. He smiled.

"I went to my fourth AA meeting last night," he said. "I'm working again. I've got a place to live."

"That's great news," I said, meaning it. I hadn't expected as much. "You made my day."

He cleared his throat and looked at the floor. "I wanted to thank you."

"Only you can change your life."

"Yeah, but I wanted to show you that I could stop drinking."

"How many weeks?"

"Six," he said.

"Good." I nodded my head encouragingly. One bender would send him back to detox, but he knew that. "I'm proud of you."

He beamed as if that's what he wanted to hear.

I met Sally for lunch at Mary's. She looked at me across the table and said, "You look beat."

"Did you take a look at Mona?"

"I sent her home. Did you have an all-night session of cribbage or something?"

"She woke me up around four, sure that Shawn doesn't love her. I don't know if that's true, but I think he's having second thoughts about getting married."

"It's not too late," she said, her eyes on mine.

The waiter brought us our soup and bread and left us alone. I hardly tasted it. "Want to stay over Friday and Saturday nights?"

"With your parents and Craig and his wife? No thanks."

"Do I detect a little internalized homophobia?" I tore off a piece of bread. Perhaps sustenance would give me more energy. I felt drained.

"Probably."

"Promise me you'll come to the reception right after work."

"I'll be there by five." She smiled, and I realized I loved her.

I leaned forward and whispered the words.

Her smile broadened, lighting up her face. "Me too."

That afternoon I rushed into the airport a few minutes before the scheduled arrival. Mona stood just outside the security gates. Through the windows a United Express plane landed on the runway and taxied toward the airport.

Mona looked better than she had at dawn. "Did you get some sleep?" I asked.

"Hops and I lay down for a while." She gave me a smile that disappeared as quickly as it came. "How come you're so late?"

"Busy day."

"What's the weather going to be tomorrow?"

"I don't know."

"It has to be nice. Everybody can't get inside."

"Let's not worry about it."

"I'm worried. I wonder if we'll have more people than we invited."

"Why would that happen?"

"Are you sure we're scheduled with the judge? I probably should have done that myself."

"I'm sure," I said, my eyes on the hall behind the barrier that led to the gates, all seven of them.

"Maybe I should call the caterers again."

"Go ahead if it'll make you feel better." The first people off the plane were walking toward us. I wondered if I would immediately recognize our parents.

And then there they were, grayer, browner, and thinner than I remembered. They looked like a commercial for retirement living. "It's them," I said.

"I know. I just saw them, remember? I hope they haven't made the trip for nothing."

"Everything will go as planned," I assured her. A smile spread over my face. "Mom, Dad." I waved and gave a little hop.

When they came through the barriers, I melted into my

mother, wondering how I'd managed to get by without her these two years. She cupped my face in her hands.

"It's so good to see you." Short wavy hair framed her face, softening the lines that creased her skin. Her hazel eyes smiled warmly. She smelled wonderful as she always did.

"Let me hug my oldest girl." Dad bulled his way to embrace me. His eyes, nearly lost in a sea of wrinkles, looked very blue against his tan. He put an arm around me and we walked toward the luggage carousels.

"You look like you spend all your days outside," I said.

"Mornings and late afternoons. The sun's too intense for midday golf."

Mona and Mom walked ahead of us, arms crossed over their backs. Mona talked nonstop into Mom's ear.

"Oh, honey, I know you've done all you can. It will be a fabulous wedding and reception," Mom said.

Mom and Dad moved up to the luggage belt, while Mona and I stood behind ready to help.

"Shawn should be here meeting Mom and Dad."

"He'll meet them when we get home."

"He wasn't there when I called a few minutes ago."

"Maybe he's out in the sunporch."

She hit her forehead with the heel of her hand. "I left the bunny out there this morning. I hope she doesn't escape. Those screens don't always latch."

Dad and Mom grabbed their bags off the carousel and carried them to where we stood. I took Mom's along with her arm and headed toward the exit. "Ride with me."

Mona and Dad followed, getting into her car which was parked in front of mine. The tires squealed as Mona pulled out into the driving lane.

I wasn't anxious to get home and drove at a leisurely pace. Mona's Focus disappeared from view. "You look great, Mom."

"You do too, honey, not a day over forty-two." We both laughed.

"What does that make you? Sixty-six? You're a young sixty-six."

"Oh well, I think it's true that people stay younger if they think young. Don't you?" She looked out at the lush green June landscape. We'd had a wet spring. The corn was nearly knee high already. "I forgot how green everything is."

"Do you miss it, Mom? Do you like living in a semi-arid state?"

"The desert's wonderful when it blooms, and the high temperatures never seem hot with the low humidity."

"But Arizona looks so impermanent. All those house trailers."

"Inexpensive housing. Your dad will never come back. He loves being able to play golf year-round."

"Do you?"

"No, but I like the warmth. I miss the lakes here, though. There's so little water in Arizona." She gazed out the window as the landscape rolled past. "Tell me about Shawn."

"He was Shirley when I met him."

"How can that be?" Mom said.

"You'll see. He's beautiful, and he loves her. They're a couple of soul mates in an unsympathetic world."

"How so?" Mom swung her head my way.

"They don't fit in. You know how it is with Mona, how she goes off on buying binges, how she talks till everyone runs away, how she can be annoyingly grandiose." I said nothing of her sexual appetite, which, judging from the sounds coming out of Mona and Shawn's room, was still strong.

"And Shawn?"

"He was planning a sex change operation when he met Mona. I think he still wants one, but now they're talking about having kids first." I chanced a look at Mom and thought maybe I'd gone too far. Her mouth was slightly open, her eyes wide.

She closed her mouth and stared through the windshield. "Don't tell your dad all this. He won't understand."

"I won't, Mom."

"So, how you are?" she asked brightly.

"I have a new girlfriend," I said. My lesbianism seemed ho-hum

146

next to Shawn and Mona's story. "Her name's Sally and she's an attorney."

"Really." She tried to sound enthusiastic, which made me sad for her, and me. Does every parent want boringly normal children? I wondered.

XXII

Mom and Dad stood talking with Shawn and Mona in the back-yard. I was in the sunporch, enjoying a breather from the long day. Shawn towered over Dad, and Mom cocked her head and smiled coyly at him.

When Mom excused herself, I went with her into the house. She stood inside the door, looking puzzled. "There's a rabbit in the kitchen."

"Yep. I found her in the ditch out by the road. Someone must have dumped her."

"Is she friendly?"

I squatted down to pick up Hops and handed her to my mother. "Very friendly."

Mom nodded at the litter box. "Does she use it?" The bunny's nose had gone into sniffing mode, burrowing into my mother's blouse. Mom laughed. "That tickles."

When the rabbit was near the litter box, she used it, but I'd found telltale droppings in all the rooms. They looked like M&Ms.

We took Mom's bag to her and Dad's old bedroom. She paused in the dining and living rooms to look at Mona's paint job. "Doesn't look so bad. Actually, I kind of like it."

"You should have seen it at first, but Mona's an artist of sorts." I thought of showing her the naked ladies in my room and decided against it.

Mom came up to my chin. When I hugged her, she felt fragile as if there weren't enough flesh and muscle over the bones. She was still holding the bunny when we sat on the double bed she'd shared with Dad.

"How are you and Dad?"

"Outside of being forgetful, we're okay. What little work needs doing around the place Craig handles—or the grandchildren." She sifted through her purse and came out with photos of Craig's two sons and a daughter. Her smile softened as she looked at the school pictures. "Too bad they're not coming. You haven't seen them in years."

"Guess I'll have to come out there to see them." I felt a touch of jealousy, knowing I would never be number one in the favorite sibling contest.

Mom loosened her hold on the rabbit, which plopped to the floor, then hopped off through the open door. I watched her disappear into the hall.

"If you want to move after Mona's married, I think you can do that without worry."

I laughed a little. "I could have left before." It wasn't my job to be my sister's keeper.

Mom touched my leg lightly, her fingertips cool. I stared at her hand, trying to remember what it was like when she and Dad had been responsible for me. Even as a child, though, I'd looked after Mona. When she told everyone in the playground she could fly and climbed the jungle gym to demonstrate, I dragged her down to safety, whispering in her ear, "You can't give away your identity," as if she were Superwoman in disguise.

"I may move in with Sally," I said.

Mom nodded as if in sympathy, but I wasn't fooled. Mom had never taken my relationships seriously, or was that my own internalized homophobia?

"I'm looking forward to meeting Sally."

"She'll be here tomorrow."

Shawn fixed drinks for everyone when we went downstairs. I mouthed, "Mona too?" and he nodded, mouthing back, "A little one."

Mona was leaning on Dad, her head on his shoulder. "My daddy," she said demurely. I winced. She'd seldom called him daddy, not that I remembered anyway.

"What do you want me to do, Shawn?" Mona and I were the sous chefs. Shawn was grilling steaks for dinner.

"Mona's making the soup. You can bake some potatoes and put together a salad. How does that sound?"

"Good." I decided to make twice-baked potatoes. This was a special occasion.

Mona stirred the soup on the stove, minestrone. She began slicing garlic bread to put in the oven. I cleaned the potatoes and nuked them in the microwave, then tore and washed spinach for salad. Mom helped me cut up green and red peppers.

We were ready to sit down to dinner in the sunporch in less than an hour. The sun, low in the west, shone in my eyes. I put on sunglasses. "Looks great, Shawn," I said, sawing at the tough steak.

The bunny sat hunched under the table, eating pieces of spinach off Dad's fingertips. It's nose quivered. "Dad, you never let us feed the dog under the table."

"One of the joys of being a grandparent is being able to do the things you told your kids not to."

"Is Hops your grandchild?"

He lifted a shoulder sheepishly. "I don't see any other progeny lurking about."

Where I might have been hurt, I chose to laugh. "Hear that, Hops? This is your grandpa."

"Shawn and I'll give you the real thing. Nine months, tops," Mona said.

"No rush," Dad remarked. "I've got three already."

I experienced a moment of temporary insanity when I thought Sally and I should produce a child—artificially inseminated or adopted. We had choices, too. Then I came to my senses. No amount of sibling rivalry could force me into motherhood. One shouldn't have children to please anyone but oneself.

Mom looked at her food and said nothing.

The next morning, the day of the wedding, we were up early. We shuffled into the kitchen one at a time, like a play, each getting a cup, filling it with coffee, and joining Mom and Dad in the sunporch.

Dad was wearing his old bathrobe, which I'd put back in his room. Mom held Hops in her lap and crooned softly into her large, twitching ears. I thought the bunny made a great pet. Her one downfall was the tiny hardened turds left randomly throughout the house.

Shafts of sunlight reached the sunporch, cross-sectioning Mom and Shawn and Dad. Mom looked up. She was wearing a sweatshirt over her pajamas. "Your outdoors feels like our air-conditioned indoors. I'm always cold."

"You'd be cold if it were a hundred degrees, Peg," Dad said dismissively.

"When are Craig and Barbara arriving?" Mom asked.

"Eleven thirty," I said. "We've got lots of time."

I was leaning against a corner post. The early morning air smelled damp and sweet. Already it was in the mid-seventies, promising a hot day.

"I'm going to start my own interior painting business," Mona announced out of the blue. "I offered my services to Dennis and he seemed interested, didn't he, Shawn?"

We stared at her as if she'd said she was going to become a top-less dancer. Shawn cleared his throat. "Yes, he did."

"Have you advertised?"

"I thought I'd wait till after the wedding. I'll specialize in sponge, rag, and feather painting. I'm pretty good, if I do say so myself."

This was typical Mona. A brief vision came to me of her buying gallons of paint, which then sat around unopened. "Get some jobs before you invest in anything."

"Look on the bright side for once, Abby. I'm tired of doing the peon work in the law firm. If I quit, they'll find out how valuable I was."

"First things first," Dad said, "and that's the wedding."

I went to the airport with Mom to meet Craig and Barbara.

"Craig's put on some weight," Mom said as we looked out the windows facing the runways, waiting for the plane to touch down.

"Haven't we all," I remarked, although Mona hadn't.

"Don't say anything. He's sensitive," she continued.

"Mom, I'm a therapist. You think I'm going to tell him he's fat?"

When he lumbered down the corridor next to Barbara, who looked tiny next to him, I murmured, "You weren't kidding."

"Shhh," she said as if they could hear us.

"Hey, sis. Looking good." Craig enfolded me in his bulk, pressing my nose and mouth against his immense chest.

"Do we have to have a wedding to get you here?" I asked, turning to hug Barbara. "How are the kids?"

"Involved. You remember how that is," Craig remarked. "When they get to be teenagers, they don't want to go anywhere with their parents. Seriously, they're on wilderness trips that were paid for before the wedding announcement."

"Luggage?" I asked.

"We checked one bag." Craig put an arm around me as we headed toward the two luggage carousels. He looked around. "Nice little airport."

"They're working on it."

"How's Mona? Excited?"

"I guess." We'd have to rush home and change for the four o'clock wedding.

"Second time around for her. She didn't say anything about marrying someone when she was visiting."

"That's 'cause she'd just met him," I said.

"A quick romance, huh? When are you going to take the plunge?"

"Craig, that's a sensitive question," Barbara protested.

"Oh, I don't mind," I said, unable to believe they didn't at least suspect why I'd never married. "I'll introduce you to my latest tonight."

"Can't wait," Craig boomed.

We stowed the one bag in the tailgate of my Saturn and got in. Craig climbed in the front with me, and the car tilted under his bulk.

"I'm looking foward to seeing the old homestead," he said.

We sped through the green countryside. Fields of corn and alfalfa flashed past. I was a little worried about getting to the courthouse in time.

As it was, I needn't have been concerned. The waiting room held two other couples and their attendants. The judge was still in court with other matters.

I'd worn a suit, as planned. Mom and Barbara and Shawn's mother had donned summery dresses. Mona was in a calf-length off-white dress, looking like a bride, albeit an older one. The men all wore light-colored suits. We were a colorful bunch. I wondered if the judge would take the couples all together.

When Judge Neff entered, I didn't think he recognized me. Then he nodded and smiled in my direction. I'd spent several hours in his courtroom during detention hearings. "This is your family?" he asked.

"Yes. My sister, Mona, is the bride."

He offered to marry the couples separately. We crowded into

his chambers where Mona and Shawn signed the wedding certificate Neff's assistant produced.

The vows were brief and without any accompanying advice, after which the bride and groom gave each other a peck on the mouth. Neff shook hands all around, and wished the couple a long and happy marriage, after which we left.

Shawn drove Mona home in his truck. Mom and Barbara rode with me, and Dad and Craig took Mona's Focus. Sally's BMW and Nance and Dennis's Lincoln were parked in our driveway, along with the caterer's van.

I showed the caterers into the kitchen, then went out to the sunporch where Sally, Nance, and Dennis were waiting. They rose to their feet to kiss Mona and congratulate Shawn, who looked pale under his tan. I smiled encouragingly at him. His mother and father looked absolutely delighted.

"We're so happy with Mona," his mother said to my mother.

"So are we with Shawn," Mom gushed in reply. She was amazed and confused, I knew. How could he be so handsome and want to change his sex? As far as she was concerned, Mona had pulled off a coup.

Taking Sally by the hand, I trailed my mother inside. She was following the rabbit turds into the living room when we caught up with her.

Surprised at how difficult this was to say, I cleared my throat. "Mom, this is my girlfriend, woman friend actually, Sally Schmidt."

Mom looked Sally in the eye. "You were Mona's friend in high school, weren't you? And now you're her employer. Abby told me you're an attorney." She sidestepped any confrontation with my sexuality.

"Yes," Sally replied, smiling. She looked luscious, dressed in a tailored pantsuit that showed off her slim figure. Her brown eyes snapped with humor, her thick hair frizzed a little from the humidity. "How nice to see you again."

"Ah, there she is." Mom threw up her hands in glee. The bunny was crouched under an end table, its nose and ears quivering. The influx of people must have frightened her.

Pulling a tissue out of my suit pocket, I began collecting rabbit turds. This wouldn't do. We couldn't have bunny doo-doo all over the house. It was unsanitary.

My cell phone rang from inside my purse, which I'd set on the couch. I pulled it out. It was Sharon.

"What is it?" I asked, annoyed at being interrupted on a vacation day.

"He's out again. Brume. He escaped when they were taking him to the hospital. He faked severe abdominal cramps."

"Has anyone notified Elizabeth?" A visual image of her clutching her purse flashed through my mind.

"The police are watching her place of employment. They'll follow her home and stay there. Thought you'd like to know, though."

"Did you tell Tracy?"

"Of course. She's going over to see Anna."

"Good. Keep me informed, will you? Call my home phone." I was abandoning my purse and suit jacket. It was hot.

XXIII

Mom clutched the rabbit to her chest. "She's afraid, poor thing." White hairs clung to her dress.

My brother came into the room, and I introduced Sally as my girlfriend. A good-looking man despite his weight, Craig was blessed with a head of thick, graying hair, large blue eyes, and a dark tan.

"You were Mona's best friend in high school, weren't you? Kind of shy then, but real smart."

"She's an attorney," Mom said. "Mona works for her."

"Is that so? You just don't look like a lawyer," Craig boomed. I was trying to remember if his voice had grown with his size or if it had always been that sonorous.

Sally smiled pleasantly. "How does a lawyer look?"

"Don't ask, honey. My experience with attorneys isn't good."

"What do you do, Craig?" Sally asked.

"I teach tech ed at the high school. Repairing small engines, building storage sheds, that sort of stuff. I love the kids."

"They love him, too," Barbara said, standing beside her husband.

I rolled the turds up in the tissue, took it to the downstairs bathroom, and flushed it down the toilet. Maybe I could talk Mom into taking the rabbit home, but I knew I'd meet stiff resistance from Mona and Dad.

When Craig and Mom and Barbara went into the dining room where the servers were laying food on the table, I told Sally Brume had escaped. He was still a sore point between us.

"Damn," she said heatedly. "How's Elizabeth?"

"I don't know. The police are watching the Shopko where she works. They'll follow her back to her apartment and keep an eye on the place."

"Do you want to go?"

"Nothing I can do. The phone worker's going to keep in touch. Maybe you should call your partner?" Sarcasm edged my tone.

"I should." She pulled out her cell phone and punched in some numbers.

I went into the dining room and filled a plate with vegetables and dip, then made my way outside, smiling and nodding. The kitchen and sunporch teemed with guests.

Shawn stood by his truck, sucking on a cigarette and talking to Dennis.

"I didn't know you smoked," I said, walking over.

"I quit three years ago," Shawn replied.

"He's got wedding remorse," Dennis explained.

Shawn covered his face with one large hand. "I'm a fool."

"Well, you're a married fool now," I reminded him. "You can't get out of it today." I was afraid he might take off, but his truck was hemmed in on all sides.

"We could get it annulled."

"Tomorrow you could, but Mona wouldn't handle it well."

"I know."

I'd already told him it was a nutty idea to begin with, even to me who was used to crazy ideas. "You've been living together. How is this so different?"

He drew himself up straight. "It's sort of permanent."

"Were the kids Mona's idea?"

Dennis's eyes followed the conversation. I threw him a glance, and he raised a hand. "I won't tell anyone, not even Nance."

"I love kids, but I don't think the two of us would make the best parents," Shawn admitted.

"Probably not." Out of the corner of my eye, I caught Mona striding toward us. She looked worried.

"What are you doing? Hiding out here?" she asked.

"Just talking," Shawn mumbled.

"Come on inside." She tugged on Shawn's arm.

"Sally's looking for you," she said to me as her heels wobbled across the gravel.

"Isn't life fun?" I said.

Dennis squeezed my shoulder. "Well, it isn't boring anyway."

"I could stand a little boring."

"Come on, girl. Let's go inside. Nance will be looking for me. That's what it's like, being attached to someone. No wonder Shawn is having second thoughts."

"That's not why and you know it." I slipped an arm through his. "You're a comfort, Dennis, do you know that?"

"Glad to be of service."

"Do you think he'll run out on her?" I felt the full heat of the sun as we moved into its glare.

"Sooner or later. Don't you?"

"Probably." Marriage didn't hold people together anymore. In a way, it was a good thing to be able to change.

Sally sat on the couch in the living room with Nance, both eating appetizers off paper plates. We stopped on the way and filled up plates for ourselves. I poured myself a glass of red wine.

"Any calls?" I asked Sally.

"Not that I know of."

"Did you get hold of Don?"

"Yes. He knew. They haven't found him."

I'd been foolishly hoping that Brume would be captured while I was outside. Sipping the wine, I sat between Sally and Nance.

"Where were you?" Nance asked Dennis.

"Outside, talking to Shawn."

"What a handsome man," she remarked.

"Prettier than me?" Dennis grinned.

"God, yes," she said.

Around ten, the guests began clearing out. All the windows were open yet the house was stifling, as hot and humid as if it were noon.

I put a hand on Sally's arm. Brume had not been found, but the police were watching Elizabeth's apartment. She and Anna were safely inside.

"Stay," I said.

She shook her head and gave me a small smile. "I'll come back for brunch tomorrow." Family and close friends, like Sally and Nance and Dennis, were invited.

We walked to her car in the damp heat. "Can we go to the cabin next weekend?" We hadn't been there since Memorial Day. I needed a getaway.

Mona and Shawn had left earlier in Mona's Focus for the Holiday Inn, where they would spend the night, returning in the morning. Shawn's parents had departed shortly after the newlyweds. Soon there would be only me, my parents, Craig and his wife.

"I offered the cabin to Mona and Shawn for their honeymoon." She stood with one foot inside the car, the other hand on top of the door, ready to slip inside.

"You didn't tell me."

"I hadn't gotten around to it, is all. I've got a ton of work. Let's spend the weekend together, though. I feel like I've hardly seen you since Mona and Shawn decided to get married."

The caterers were packing up to leave. They'd stuffed our fridge with enough food to last for days. I sat down in the sunporch along with Mom, Dad, Craig, and Barbara. A June bug buzzed against the screen door.

"Nice party," Craig said. His shirt was unbuttoned at the neck, his tie gone, rolls of flesh coiled around his neck. "Whew, I'd forgotten how hot summer nights can be here."

"I love them," I said.

"You should move to Arizona," Craig suggested.

I shook my head. "Not for me."

"Shawn seemed like a really nice guy, and so handsome," Barbara remarked. "How did Mona meet him?"

"He redid the woodwork in the house," I told her.

The bunny huddled under a chair like a silent, white ghost. "Maybe I should take her home with me," Mom said, picking her up.

"It's all right with me, but you'll have to tear her away from Mona."

"Well, it's not okay with me," Dad said. "She drops turds everywhere. Haven't you noticed?"

"Excuse me a minute." I went into the kitchen to call Elizabeth.

The phone rang four times before the answering machine picked up. I listened to Elizabeth's brief message and began to leave my own. "This is Abby Dean. I'm wondering . . ."

"Hello, hello." It was Elizabeth. The police had probably told her to screen her messages. "Abby?"

"I'm here."

"He's out there somewhere, looking for me." Her voice quavered with fear. "It's impossible to get rid of him."

I was thinking that myself. "The police are outside the door. Right? Hang in there. You'll be safe." I gave her my phone number and told her to call whenever she wanted to talk.

Mom's eyes followed me as I let myself into the porch. "Sally?" she asked.

I shook my head. "Work." I felt helpless. All we could do was sit around and wait for Brume to pounce.

The next day Mona and Shawn showed up around ten. They parked behind the caterer's van, the first to arrive. Mona looked excited, as if she were bursting with news. Shawn appeared tired and out of sorts. Sally crunched down the driveway shortly afterwards with Nance and Dennis on her tail. I'd gone out to the garage to get orange juice out of the extra fridge and stood in the open doorway, grinning.

"It's so hot, I wore shorts. Hope you don't mind," Sally said, hopping out of the BMW. "I brought a change of clothes in case you do." Sally had great legs. She looked radiant, rested and happy. I felt a rush of desire.

"I love you in shorts. You can wear them anytime as far as I'm concerned." I waved at Dennis and Nance as they parked next to Sally's car and got out.

"Dennis has to leave right after brunch. Can you give me a lift home, Sally?" Nance asked.

"Sure."

"Wait a minute. I don't want her to go home," I put in.

"I've got work to do, Abby." She gave me an apologetic smile.

"The caterers are in the kitchen," I said.

Mona handed us a computer-generated flyer of a woman sponge-painting a wall, pink on white. Other available applications were listed under the picture. At the bottom of the page, it read *Artistic Work at Reasonable Prices* along with Mona's name and phone number.

"I did this at the office this morning. Hope you don't mind, Sally. We bought some paint, so I'm ready to go."

"Of course not," Sally said.

Arms crossed, Shawn stood by quietly. "That's how we spent the first morning of our honeymoon."

"I'm going to show this to Dennis." Mona flounced off.

I helped the caterers put the food, utensils, glasses, and plates on the dining room table. People could sit where they wanted. Sally and I sat on the living room couch with Nance and Barbara, using the coffee table to hold our plates.

Mona still had Dennis cornered. She filled her plate as he did his, all the time talking.

161

"Maybe I should go rescue him," I said.

"From what?" Barbara asked.

"Naw, he's a big boy. He can take care of himself," Nance said.

Dennis looked our way and crossed his eyes. I laughed. Mona tugged on his arm.

"I'm serious about this. I'm good, too."

"I know, I know," he said hastily, and sat down at the dining room table. She took the chair next to his.

I smiled at Nance. "He's a doll."

Barbara looked confused, but I wasn't about to explain Mona to her.

XXIV

Mom and Dad flew out Sunday on the same plane as Craig and Barbara.

I felt both bereft and relieved as the plane taxied away from the airport, lifted into the sky, and turned toward Chicago, their first leg of the trip. Bereft because I so seldom saw my parents and brother. Relieved because now life could go back to normal.

Mom hadn't taken the bunny, even though I told her the kennel would fit under the plane seat. Dad had said no rabbit was going to poop all over his house.

Mona and Shawn had left for a weeklong honeymoon at Sally's cabin. She was staying with me while they were gone. It was a compromise of sorts. Besides, there was all the leftover food to be eaten.

I drove home from the airport, hoping she would be there to greet me, but only the bunny waited in the kitchen. Hops was in her box, kicking litter all over the floor with her powerful hind legs. I should take her to the humane society and exchange her for a dog, I thought. Dad was right in not wanting a pet that crapped all over the house. Instead, I picked her up and held her to my chest, where I dripped hot tears on her white fur.

I spun around at Sally's rap on the kitchen door, foolishly fearing it might be Brume.

"Hi, girlfriend," I said.

"Why are you crying?" Sally wiped the tears away with a hand. "Put that rabbit down and come here."

I moved into her arms and sniffled as she kissed the wet trails on my cheeks. We ended upstairs, shedding clothes on the floor and falling on the bed in passionate embrace.

We slid against each other, moving in sweaty, sensuous rhythm. In the weeks we'd been lovers, we'd learned how to please each other.

Afterwards, I crawled into her arms and lay panting.

"If you lived with me, we could do this whenever we liked."

"Sex loses its urgency with availability." My eyes strayed to the naked ladies. I would hate to leave them behind. Actually, I wasn't sure I wanted to give up the independence of living in my own house, even if I had to share it with Mona and Shawn.

On Monday after the staff meeting, I was paged to the reception room where Elizabeth Halbertson waited. A policeman, who was leafing through *Sports Illustrated*, accompanied her. Brume was still at large, but I figured that by now he'd skipped town.

"Come on in, Elizabeth."

In my office, she sat on the edge of a chair, gripping her purse, as if ready to run.

"What's happening?" I asked. A silly question under the circumstances, but it was how I usually started my sessions.

Looking at her lap, she said quietly, "I sent him a note. I don't know why I felt sorry for him, but I did."

164

All the weeks of therapy shot to hell, I thought, and the case against Brume compromised. "You felt sorry for him?" I repeated.

She shrugged fatalistically. "He wasn't all bad. I think he loved me. He didn't mean to hurt me. He was cornered."

I looked out the skinny window at the courthouse lawn. "So it's okay for him to hold you hostage at gunpoint? How do you define love, Elizabeth?"

"He said he didn't want to live without me." A whisper.

"He also said he didn't want you to live without him. Isn't that what you told me?"

"Yes." A murmur.

"Does he know where you live?"

"No." She looked up, her eyes tear-filled.

"Good. Are you scared?"

"To death," she said.

Shouts from somewhere—down the hall—through a door. No one had ever yelled while I was here, not with such urgency.

"It's him." Looking terrified, she half-rose out of her chair.

A gunshot reverberated through the confines of the building, followed by screams and more shouts. I flinched as if hit. This couldn't be happening, I thought, not with a cop in the waiting room. I jumped to my feet, put a hand on the doorknob, and then backed away from it. A bullet could penetrate easily, and there was no lock.

Elizabeth's gaze moved frantically around the room, searching for escape.

"Under the computer desk," I said. There were two desks in my office, the one I'd always had and the one that came with the computer.

She fell to her knees and crawled into the opening. I dropped back in my chair, my eyes on the door, waiting for the next shot. The first had given me an instant headache. Unable to decide whether to crawl under the other desk or go out into the hallway to see what was going on, I stayed put—frozen with fear. I heard footsteps on the other side of the door. My heart hammered loudly.

I thought of the many bosses and co-workers shot and killed by disgruntled former employees. It made more sense, though, to think Brume was here, looking for Elizabeth.

The doorknob turned. I held my breath. "You all right, Abby?" Mark asked, tapping on and then opening the door.

I jumped to my feet, and my legs nearly collapsed. My teeth chattered. "What's going on?"

"James Brume shot a policeman in the waiting room, and ran. They'll catch him." Elizabeth crawled out from under the desk. "Ah," he said. "Now it makes sense."

Ashamed by how frightened I was, I fell weakly onto my chair and scowled angrily at Elizabeth. Not for bringing Brume here, but for writing to him, for giving him hope.

I hadn't recognized the policeman and finally thought to ask, "How is he? The officer?"

"He was bundled off to the hospital. I don't think the wound is serious." Bob looked over Mark's shoulder, and Debbie pushed her way to the front.

"We need another policeman here. Now. To escort Elizabeth home."

Elizabeth got to her feet and ran shaky fingers through her hair. She met my eyes and glanced away. "I'm sorry," she said.

"Hey, it's not your fault," Debbie assured her, taking Elizabeth by the arm and bustling her down the hall to the phone workers' room to wait for a police escort.

The door to the hall that led from the waiting room to our offices opened. It was kept locked. Maybe that's what saved us. Four cops bustled through it. I felt reassured by their presence.

An officer questioned me in my office. My hands were shaking. I told him I'd seen nothing, had only heard the gunshot. I'd been talking to Brume's ex-girlfriend at the time and, yes, she'd told me she'd sent him a note. She realizes she made a mistake.

"Don't I know you?" He was young.

"You've probably seen me in the emergency room or the jail." I clenched my hands tightly, to hide the shaking.

When he left, I looked out the window. The area in front of the courthouse teemed with police. Their headquarters were just down the street.

Tracy knocked on my door. "What about Anna?" she said worriedly.

"I assume Anna's at the apartment, safely locked behind the door."

"She doesn't answer the phone. Of course, that's nothing new. I'll go check up on her."

I wondered if Brume had a grudge against Anna, if he'd recognize her as the one who'd hit him over the head. "The police are taking Elizabeth there now." I'd seen her leave with them.

I crossed the hall to Mark's open office. Bob and Debbie were there, all of them rehashing Brume's assault, talking about how scared they were. I told them that Elizabeth had contacted Brume. It made me wonder, as I had many times before, if any attempt to change learned behavior was successful. Maybe we were all set on a fateful course under the influence of our parents.

"Do you ever feel as if you're wasting your time here?" I asked.

"All too often," Debbie said.

"You're not," Bob assured us with youthful energy. "Think of all the people you've helped."

Mark met my eyes. "He might have broken in whether she'd written to him or not. Maybe he saw her entering the building from his cell."

I sat down. All appointments were canceled for the rest of the day. We chatted, while fellow workers wandered in and out. If this were a school or some other place of work, one of us would be called in to counsel those traumatized. Instead, we talked to each other, trying to come to terms with our feelings.

I was on call all day. My loss of faith was again corroborated when Karl Jankowski, so drunk as to be comatose, showed up at the emergency room.

Carol Watkins told me he'd passed out in a bar. I nodded.

"Karl, wake up," I said.

"Whadsha want?" He raised his eyes, his head swaying on its stalk of a neck. "Oh, it'sh you. My wife ish sheeing shomeone elshe. My kidsh hate me. What'sh the point." His chin dropped to his chest. "They don't need me."

"I'll talk to him when he's sober. Better put him in detox."

After work, I stopped at Elizabeth's, arriving in time to watch coverage of the policeman carried out of the Human Services building on a gurney on the local news. A photo of James Brume filled the screen. We were told he was driving a black Dodge pickup, that he was armed and dangerous.

"That's the man I knocked over the head," Anna said. "Too bad I didn't kill him."

I put a hand on her on the shoulder and she shrank from my touch. It wasn't personal, I knew. It was the disease, but still the rejection bothered me. "Somebody will spot him," I said, meaning to be reassuring.

"The cops won't stop him," Elizabeth said. "He'll get to me. Maybe I'll be glad. I'm going crazy, cooped up in here. I can't even go to a movie."

She looked at me and I saw anger in her eyes. "All those cops and they couldn't even catch him."

I felt anger of my own. "If he contacts you, you'll tell them, won't you?"

She dropped her gaze. "Of course."

"I'm going now. If you need me, you have my phone number."

I nodded to the two policemen who sat in their squad car outside the apartment. The late afternoon sun hid behind haze, while thunderclouds piled up in the east. The breeze smelled of rain.

I drove home, keeping my eyes peeled for Dodge pickups. The blacktop unrolled under my tires, softened by heat.

XXV

At home there was a message on the machine from Sally. She wouldn't be coming out tonight. She had to prepare for a court appearance the next day.

The bunny hopped into the kitchen and over to my feet. She was breathing heavily, probably because it was so hot in the house. I went around throwing open windows and turning on fans. To hell with Brume being on the loose and dangerous. Why would he come here?

I patted Hops while filling her water and food bowls. Then I phoned Sally at work. She answered on the first ring.

"I'm sorry, Abby. They moved a court date up."

"Did you hear about what happened at Human Services today?"

"No. I've been holed up in my office. What?"

I told her, and she sounded alarmed, "Are you all right?"

"*I* am," I said.

"I'll come if you need me, even if I have to go to court unprepared."

"No. Forget it. I'm okay. I've got Hops to keep me company." Even as I protested, I knew I wasn't all right with it. Knowing that I'd do the same if I were on call didn't make me any more willing to understand.

"I'll be there tomorrow. We can talk then."

"Sure." I hung up before I said anything more. People always expect a therapist to be understanding all the time. Only that isn't how it works. I could be as selfish as the next person. I also know how to twist an argument to my own advantage.

Putting the bunny's harness on, I took her outside for a walk. We'd done this before, letting her graze in the yard and garden. Tying her to a stake where she could nibble the tomatoes that grew in such profusion, I sat in the sunporch and read the newspaper.

It was early evening when I heard the scream and saw the rabbit, leash trailing, lifted skyward by a barred owl. Rushing out of the porch, I jumped for the end of the leash. The owl, who apparently wasn't up to carrying so much weight, dropped the rabbit, Bending over Hops, who was making small, frightened noises, I saw the gashes where the owl's talons had pierced skin and flesh. Blood leaked onto the white coat.

Wrapping Hops in a towel, I rushed her to the vet, knowing someone was always on call. The bunny's eyes closed on the stainless steel examining table.

The vet, a white-coated middle-aged man, shook his head when I told him what had happened. His fingers moved gently over the rabbit. "Its spine is broken," he concluded.

I stared at the closed eyes, the quivering pink nose, the flattened ears, and nodded. "You'll have to put her down."

"It's not a terrible thing," he said, meeting my eyes with sympathy.

It wasn't. I kept a comforting hand on the rabbit as the injection did its fatal work. Hops's nose stopped quivering, her eyes opened once and then closed again, and her body relaxed as if in sleep. The vet handed me a tissue. I'd hardly known this rabbit, but it was more the way animals handle fate, including their own deaths, that moved me to tears. They always seemed to know when to stop fighting or running, and died without complaint.

I left Hops on the examining table and went out the door. I noticed nothing on the way home except what was etched into my brain—the rabbit on the examining table. Once there I flopped down in the sunporch. The western sky was smeared with yellow. Clouds continued to pile up in the east and spread westward. Thunder rumbled. It would rain soon.

The phone rang as the last of the light faded. I realized I hadn't eaten.

"Where have you been?" Nance demanded

"An owl got the rabbit. I had to have her put down." I began crying.

"How did that happen?"

"I tied her in the garden. The owl dropped her. I guess she was too heavy."

"I'm sorry." Nance's voice softened. "I was worried about you. I saw the news. Were those your offices where that poor policeman was shot?"

"Yes."

"You've had a really bad day, sweetie. Is Sally with you?"

"No. She has a court case tomorrow to get ready for." I was feeling sorry for myself, something I tried not to do.

"I'll come over," Nance said.

"Is that okay with Dennis?"

She scoffed. "Do I need permission?"

I returned to the sunporch with a drink in hand. Lightning streaked across the sky, followed by crashes of thunder. The air was hot, thick, and dense with moisture. I sat down to watch nature's display and wait for Nance.

Headlights bobbed up the driveway and came to a halt in front of the garage. Nance climbed out of her Lincoln and walked toward the porch lights. She wore shorts and a tank top. Her hair was pulled back from her face and neck in a ponytail.

"Aren't you even going to give me a hug, honey?" she asked, setting down her overnight bag.

I sighed heavily and got to my feet. "You're a good friend, Nance."

"Good friends beget good friends," Nance replied, kissing the air next to my cheek. Her body was comforting against mine.

She sat down in one of the cushioned lounge chairs. "Where are your manners, girl. Aren't you going to offer me whatever you're drinking?"

"You're not picky anyway." I went into the kitchen with her on my heels and refilled my drink before fixing her one.

"Do you think we're safer inside?" she asked.

I thought she was referring to the lightning. "It's so pretty, though. I want to watch. We'll come in when the rains start."

"I was thinking about this man on the loose."

"Oh. I don't think he'll come here. I don't think he connects me with Elizabeth." I looked at her. "How are you and Dennis?" I was remembering her brief marital indiscretion.

Nance waved dismissively. "Talk to me." She took a long swig and trained her gaze on me.

"It would break my heart if you two broke up." I was sounding a little sappy.

"We won't. Trust me. Now let's hear from your side."

"I feel like a failure at work and at home. Work sucks, and I let an owl kill the bunny."

"Mona's wedding went well." She let out a little shriek as lightning streaked to earth, followed by a loud boom.

I pulled myself upright in the chaise longue. "I couldn't stop that either."

Nance shrugged and pulled herself closer together. "Shawn's gorgeous."

"Gorgeous, smorgeous." The vodka on an empty stomach went immediately to my head. "He wants to be a woman. Mona will fall

172

apart." It wouldn't matter that Mona knew this from the beginning. She said she'd support him. I'd hold her to it.

"Look, honey, it makes me nervous to be out here, waiting to be fried alive."

Just then the rain broke loose and a cool breeze kicked up, sweeping it our way. I closed the doors on the porch and we went inside.

Sally crept into my bedroom during the night. I sat upright, heart pounding, not completely sure that it wasn't Brume.

"Who is it?" I asked weakly.

"Shhh. It's me. Sally." She slid into bed in her shorts and tank top. Her hair and body dripped rain.

I put my arms around her. "I thought you weren't coming."

She smoothed my hair away from my face and kissed me with wet lips.

"The bunny's dead," I said, crying softly into her neck. I told her about the owl. I was responsible.

"I'm sorry, sweetie. That's a shame, but you rescued her once and gave her a few good weeks. Whose car is out there? I nearly went back home."

"Nance's."

"She's a better friend than I am." Sally kissed me again.

"She didn't have a house to sell. Nothing stood in her way. That's how it is. I forgive you."

She kissed my breasts, and I thought that as long as there was passion, we'd be okay.

We fell asleep in a tangle of arms and legs and awoke when the radio came on. On the way to the bathroom, I noticed Nance's bedroom door was open, the bed neatly made. Downstairs, her note on the kitchen table read,

Have an eight-thirty appointment. Will call later.

I made coffee and oatmeal. When Sally came downstairs, breakfast was on the table.

"I could live like this," she said.

"Your turn tomorrow. No reason to stay here now that the rabbit's gone. I'll come to your house after work."

I locked the house and left without looking back. Usually, I was a little obsessive—rechecking to make sure the fridge door was shut, that the water was turned off at the faucets, that the lights weren't on. I wanted to get away from the place. It felt empty and held memories of guilt.

During the morning staff meeting we talked about Brume's escape and what that meant for Anna and Elizabeth. Elizabeth had rescheduled for Wednesday.

I said, "I thought we were making progress, and then she writes to the man. She's terrified of him, and she tells him she feels bad for him. It might have given him the impetus to escape."

"Well, she won't do it again," Debbie put in.

"She might." Then I told them about the rabbit. "Mona's going to have a shit fit."

"Why don't you get a dog? One too big for an owl," Mark suggested.

"And then there's Karl Jankowski, who's drinking again."

"Well, I've got one who keeps trying to kill herself. I don't know what to do with her anymore. She took half a bottle of Tylenol yesterday," Bob said.

His failure made mine pale a little.

Before I left work that day I called Sally. "Do you like dogs?"

"Doesn't everybody?" she replied.

XXVI

I met Sally at the local humane association after work. She gave me one of her uplifting smiles as she got out of the BMW, looking terrific in a gray business suit over a white shirt.

"How was court?" I asked.

"I was prepared. It went well." She walked toward me, her low heels clicking on the pavement.

I wanted to put an arm around her and pull her close. Instead, I opened the door for her. Inside, the smell of animals seeped through whatever was used to disinfect the place. Dogs barked from beyond an interior door.

"Just here to look," I said brightly.

We peered into the cages of the animals, who gazed out at us with mournful eyes. The first dog's tail wagged its entire body. It was a black Labrador mix, young and friendly. *Adoption Pending* was stamped on the informational sheet on the kennel.

The second dog, a husky mix, lay in a hair pile on the pad at the rear of the cage. It, too, had an *Adoption Pending*.

The third dog to look at us out of sorrowful eyes was ten years old—an overweight, unkempt golden retriever. Struggling to its feet, it wagged its tail slowly. Like the bunny, it had been abandoned. *Landlord* was the reason for its being here. There were apartments that took dogs, I knew.

Sally voiced what I was thinking. "Who would let their old dog go?" It was like giving away a child.

We continued down the aisle, looking in at a redbone hound mix, another young lab mix, a dachshund type, three puppies. All except the old golden had adoptions pending.

We continued on to the cat room where cats of all ages meowed in greeting. Most of their informational sheets were stamped *Adoption Pending*.

From there we went to the overflow room, where rabbits and guinea pigs and one white rat filled cages along with an overflow of cats. "I could get another rabbit, I suppose." But there were none that resembled Hops.

"I'm going to get that poor old dog," Sally said, "unless you are."

I felt a surge of love for her. "He'll shed like crazy, and he won't live long, and he'll cost you money in vet bills."

"At least he'll die happily." She looked so indignant I wanted to kiss her.

"We'll share him," I said impulsively, knowing he was not the dog I would choose ordinarily. "Think I should get another rabbit for Mona?"

"If she wants one, she can get it herself. It's not a good idea to buy someone an animal."

"You sound annoyed."

She studied me for a moment. "Mona can manage on her own. Besides, now she has Shawn."

I searched her eyes for a moment trying to reclaim my aplomb, which she'd just punched a hole in. I'd taken care of Mona as a child. When my parents left, I felt I'd been assigned that task. I couldn't let the county take over. How would that look with me on the crisis team? "Let's go take another look at the dog."

A volunteer, a stout, smiling older woman, let Goldie out of the cage. He seemed pleased to see us and stood patiently while we patted him. Hair flew off his coat, clinging to Sally's dark suit and my slacks.

Sally was looking indignant again. "How could anyone let their old dog go?"

"They couldn't afford him anymore," the volunteer said. "One of them was laid off. They have to move to a cheaper apartment that doesn't take dogs. We promised to call if we couldn't find a home for him."

"Oh. Then it isn't because they don't love him."

"No. They were all crying when they left. It nearly broke my heart."

We couldn't take him home anyway. There was a probationary period after the adoption papers were filled out, while they checked out the adopting family, which was Sally. She had no fenced-in backyard, but then neither did I.

I whispered in her ear that if this dog liked water, she might have trouble keeping him out of the river. Didn't all goldens love to swim?

We stopped for dinner at the Olive Garden. I ordered all-you-can-eat salad and garlic bread along with a vodka and tonic. I'd had some time to think. "Maybe we can reunite the dog with his family once they can afford him again."

"Think they'd tell us who they are? And what if we fall in love with him?"

I was picturing the dog in my mind. He made me sad. "Mona's going to be furious about the rabbit, you know."

"I know, but it could have happened under her watch."

"Has Don heard from Brume?"

"He's not representing Brume anymore."

"So you can tell me if he heard from him?"

"It depends."

"You are crabby tonight."

"You're right. I am. I don't know why."

"Should I go to my home?"

"No, don't. I'm sorry. I think Brume has probably skipped town."

I loved her house with all the windows open. The river gleamed beyond the backyard, hemmed in by trees, mills, and houses. In an earlier century its rapids had been dammed, transforming it into a watery highway. Now that most of the locks were closed boat traffic was limited.

On Wednesday, when Elizabeth sat down in my office, I opened with my usual, "What's happening?"

"I haven't heard from James, if that's what you're asking. My phone is tapped. I can't make a move without someone watching. It makes me nervous."

"Would you be more nervous if the police weren't there to protect you?"

"I don't know. Maybe," she said sullenly.

I was ready to throw up my hands. "I want you to think back to what it was like when James was in your life. Are you better off now than you were then?"

"Well, I don't have anyone."

"Would a boyfriend fit into your life right now?"

She looked down at her hands, clutching the purse, kneading it, and began to cry. Large drops coursed down her cheeks. She wiped them off with the heel of her hand. "I'm lonely."

I handed her a tissue. "There are lots of people out there who are just as lonely, who are in need of a friend. Ask a co-worker over to watch a video."

She sniffed. "I know I shouldn't have sent that letter. I was remembering the good times when I first met him."

I quirked an eyebrow. "Those won't come back. James has moved to another level. One of violence."

She sobbed harder. I nudged the tissue box toward her. "How's Anna? She's company, isn't she?"

Elizabeth laughed and sniffed at the same time. "She doesn't have much to say. It's like having a ghost around the place sometimes or several ghosts, when she's talking to her invisible people."

"The meds and the disorder give her a flat affect, unless, as you say, she's hearing voices."

"She laughed, though, the other day when we were watching something on TV. It was a beer commercial that ended with this black guy putting a shaggy dog on his head so that he could go into a bar that didn't let dogs in. Some woman poked the dog in the rear and it growled." Elizabeth chortled, her eyes sparkling behind the tears. "She laughs at those goose commercials, too, the AFLAC goose."

"So do I," I said with a smile. Then, "Look, I want you to think about how things were between you and James and tell me next time what you'll expect from a new boyfriend."

She blinked a couple of times and blew her nose. "Do you think there'll be another boyfriend?"

"You bet I do."

I felt a little better about her prospects after she left. I was thinking maybe there was a happy future for her after all when the phone rang.

"The family reclaimed Goldie. They decided not to move. Want to pick out another dog after work?"

I felt only relief. "You go. I'll fix dinner at your house."

I stopped at the nearest store, picked up some chicken legs and breasts, red potatoes, green leaf lettuce, and a loaf of freshly baked Italian bread. It was odd being at Sally's house alone. I turned on public radio to listen to the last half-hour of *All Things Considered*.

Brushing barbecue sauce on the chicken, I placed the pieces in a baking pan and put them in the oven. I quartered the potatoes and put them in a steamer on the stove. I could see the TV from the kitchen sink, where I tore up lettuce and sliced a red pepper I'd found in the fridge. At six I switched on the local news. A mug shot of Brume flashed on the screen.

179

I wondered how Elizabeth dealt with seeing James Brume's photo on the news every night. She'd told me Anna always said, "I hit him on the head. I should have killed him." I wished she had.

Sally arrived home around six-thirty. "No dogs, at least none I want," she said. "Let me go change clothes."

"Take your time." I was reading the paper on the porch, the TV off, the table set, the food keeping warm in the oven.

"I could get used to coming home to a hot meal," Sally said when she came downstairs.

"So could I," I said, moving food to the table. "Tell me about the Humane Society. There had to be something there."

"I nearly brought home a cat, but I didn't know if you were allergic or even liked cats."

"Bring home whatever you like. It'll be your pet." I didn't think I wanted to be tied down. Otherwise, why would I have felt so relieved when Goldie's former owners reclaimed him.

I wasn't at the house when Shawn brought Mona home on Saturday. Sally and I had gone sailing on Lake Winnebago with a friend of hers, a woman who seemed terribly knowledgeable.

Her name was Lois Tuttle, and she taught physical education at one of the local high schools. She nodded, smiled, and shook my hand when Sally introduced her as an old friend.

Lois barked commands like a real captain. The boat was a two-master with a small cabin. I knew nothing about sailing. The wind was fierce enough to scare me. Lake Winnebago is some thirty miles long and twelve miles wide, and strong winds quickly whip it into a dangerous frenzy.

"Maybe this isn't such a good idea," I said to Sally, already intimidated by Lois, who looked as if she would take on anything.

Lois threw life jackets at us. "Put these on. If you fall in, stay close to the boat." She donned one herself.

We were now away from the High Cliff marina. Lois switched off the small motor used to propel the boat away from the docks.

She and Sally raised the sails, and the wind caught them with a snap. The deck tilted and I started a slide toward the gray waves.

"Watch out," Lois yelled.

I ducked just in time as the sails slapped again and the boom swung my way. Lois pulled in the sheet and handed it to Sally as the boat leaned the other way. Lois manned the rudder. Sally and I dropped into the hole, out of the way of the boom.

The sight of white sails against blue sky was breathtaking. We skimmed across the water, powered by a hot summer wind. I threw my head back as the air rushed past. In a surprisingly short time, we neared the inlet where the Fox River leaves Lake Winnebago and begins making its way toward Green Bay.

Lois turned the rudder into the wind, called for Sally to let out the sheet, and the boat came to. Sally pulled the sails in to Lois's satisfaction, and we swept toward the east side of the lake. We had to stay out a half mile or so from shore to avoid the sandbars. I knew Winnebago was a dangerous lake in a storm. I realized now why. Its shallowness and vast expanse allowed the wind to stir it into huge waves in a short time. Its sandbars easily grounded deep-keeled boats that were blown too close to shore.

When we docked, I thanked Lois and walked to the BMW on shaky legs, giving Sally a few moments alone with her friend. I hadn't missed how they worked as a team on the sailboat. When Sally joined me, I casually mentioned this to her.

She started the engine, waved at Lois, and drove up the road out of the park. "We used to race together. I owned part of that boat at one time."

"You were lovers?"

"No. I was married."

XXVII

Mona's voice on Sally's machine punctured my short-lived freedom, even though she only said, "Call me, Abby. I'm home."

When Sally went upstairs to shower, I reluctantly picked up the receiver and punched in my home number.

Mona answered immediately, "The back door was unlocked."

I was sure I'd locked it. I remembered double-checking.

"Did you take the rabbit?" she asked.

"How was your honeymoon? Catch any fish?" Mona and Dad had been great fishing buddies. Next to hunting, she liked fishing best.

"We ate trout every day. I had to bait Shawn's hook when he bothered to throw a line in. Do you believe that?" She raised her voice as if she wanted to be heard by someone in the next room. Shawn, I presumed.

"Did you have a good time?" I ventured to ask.

"I did," she said loudly. "I don't know about Shawn. I think he got a little bored."

"Why are you shouting?" I asked, thinking about all the money they'd spent, all the guests who came to celebrate their union.

"I taught Shawn how to play cribbage. When are you coming home?"

"Monday," I said, dreading it. I clearly remembered locking the door.

"Why not tomorrow?" she asked.

"Monday," I said firmly.

"Bring Hops with you."

"Take your meds, Mona."

"Leave me alone, for chrissake," she said.

It was late in the day. I hurried a protesting Sally out the door. Her hair was still wet, and the hot wind from the BMW blew it into strands. "We just got home," she said.

"I know, but there's a white rabbit at the Humane Association. I called."

We arrived shortly before closing time. The rabbit was smaller than Hops had been. Its litter box was scattered with turds, a good sign.

"Can I have this rabbit by Monday at five?" I asked.

Apparently, they didn't have such strict rules for adopting rabbits as they did for cats and dogs. I was told that should be enough time to check up on me. I felt vaguely insulted as I filled out the forms, using Nance and Sally as references.

In the car, I said peevishly, "You'd think they'd just be grateful to find homes for all these animals."

"This way they're neutered and go to good homes. They don't turn up again as problems."

"You're right. I just don't like being screened."

"Why are you doing this?" she asked. "Why don't you tell Mona the truth?"

"She's going to need something to love."

"But why are you afraid to tell her Hops is dead?"

"Why do you care, Sally? Do you want me to make her feel bad?"

"I want you to let her grow up."

I smiled thinly. "Believe me, there's nothing I want more than an independent Mona."

She looked doubtful and sat for a moment behind the wheel without turning on the engine.

"What?" I asked.

"How is this going to work out for us?"

"I didn't think Mona was a problem with you."

"If Shawn leaves, will you feel as if you have to be there all the time?"

"Certainly not all the time." I was thinking about the unlocked door. It gave me a creepy feeling.

Mona called in the night, the sound working its way into my dream. I woke groggily when Sally answered.

"Mona. What's going on at two in the morning?" Silence. "Are you sure? Where's Shawn?" Sally turned to look at me. "Just a minute. Mona says someone's trying to break in."

Instantly awake, I grabbed the phone. "I'll call the police. Get your gun, but don't shoot anyone." I punched 911 and gave the person on call my home address, phone and cell numbers. "Someone's trying to break in."

Leaping out of bed, I pulled on the shorts and T-shirt I'd stepped out of earlier. "It's Brume. I know it is. I'm sure I locked the door when I left. It was open when Mona got home."

Sally groaned and sat up. She pulled on some clothes, I grabbed my cell phone, and we headed out the door.

"I'll drive," I said. My car was parked outside the garage, and I backed out of the driveway while still fastening my seat belt. The tires squealed as I stepped on the accelerator, but the engine balked when I pushed it.

"Don't kill us getting there," Sally warned, running her fingers through her hair. "Do you think she's imagining things, or is this a way to get you home?"

"I hope so to both," I answered.

We sped out of town onto the dark country roads. Sally said, "She's a good shot, isn't she?"

"Yes. Excellent. Even at night."

When we pulled into the driveway, the cops were already there. I parked behind the flashing lights and jumped out of the Saturn. A beater of a car was parked in front of the garage, its rusted chassis exposed in the intermittent glare.

Four people stood around a body prone on the pavement outside the back door, Shawn and Mona among them.

"Who are you?" The sheriff blocked my view. I recognized him from the signs in people's yards before his election.

"She's my sister. She works for the county. And that's my boss. She's my lawyer," Mona said.

The sheriff stepped aside and I stared down at the man. The outside light shone on his face. It wasn't Brume lying there, though. It was Karl.

"Is he alive?" I asked, almost mute with surprise.

Blood seeped through a towel wrapped around Karl's side. His skin looked gray, his eyes were closed, his breathing shallow.

"Do you know him?" a beefy deputy officer asked.

"As a matter of fact, I do. His name is Karl Jankowski." What the hell was he doing here?

The wail of the ambulance siren, at first faint, soon filled the night. A large hole was blown through the back door and screen. Luckily, Mona hadn't seen her target. She would have killed him. Her eyes looked huge in her pale face. I felt partly responsible, telling her to get her gun but not to shoot.

The lights of the ambulance flashed behind the squad cars. Three emergency technicians hurried to where we were standing. We backed away from Karl to give them room. One knelt beside him, wrapped his arm in a blood pressure cuff, and listened to his vitals. Another tightened a tourniquet around his side. The third ran to the ambulance and came back with a gurney and a bag of saline solution.

They stabilized Karl's neck and head and transferred him to the gurney. One tried to insert a needle into his hand, but the veins collapsed one after another. The EMT found a bigger vein in his arm and put a needle in it.

"Anyone know the history on this guy?" one of the med techs asked.

I said, "He's an alcoholic. He's probably over the limit right now. I don't think he abuses any other substances."

"Thought so," the guy who had just found the vein muttered.

I didn't know where Karl was staying. It looked like he'd been living at my house while Mona and I were gone.

When they carted Karl away to the ambulance, I felt as if I should follow. He'd been my client so long.

The ambulance headed toward the hospital. The rest of us went inside, where I looked for traces of Karl. I found them in my unmade bed and called the sheriff to my room.

The deputy, who came with him, began dusting for finger-prints. I stood near the door, watching, saying nothing. Once the deputy looked at the naked ladies, then at me. His already dark skin flushed.

"My sister's an artist," I said with a small smile. "She does walls. It's her new business."

Mona came to the door. "Hey, he's been in our bed, too."

"We'll be in there shortly," the sheriff said. Then to the deputy, "Hurry up there, Ben."

"Reminds me of Goldilocks and the three bears," Ben muttered.

The sheriff laughed loudly. "He's a funny guy, ain't he? That's why I keep him around."

"Do you know how to take fingerprints?" I wasn't in the mood for humor.

"Yes, but we only have the one kit." Nevertheless, he took the hint and began helping.

Sally appeared in the doorway, looking pale and tired, her hair tousled. This was going to be a long night, but we could sleep late the next day.

Light was filtering into the sky when the sheriff and his deputy left. Mona went upstairs with Shawn to change her sheets and go to bed.

"Let's stay here tonight," I said. "I've had it."

Sally shrugged. We changed our sheets and tumbled onto them. Although I ached with weariness, I lay awake listening to Sally's soft breathing. A mild breeze thick with moisture flowed through the screen. With it came the smell of fresh-cut hay.

The idea of Karl living in the house spooked me. It was too coincidental that one of my clients should move into my place. I'd find out if he knew it was my home, that is if he recovered from the gunshot wound.

Hearing someone out in the hallway and then downstairs, I got up. Sure it was Mona, nevertheless I snuck down the steps. She was in the kitchen, looking at the door. Shawn had nailed a piece of scrap lumber over the hole.

"Think they'll put me in jail?" she asked, turning to face me. She looked ghastly—white-faced with dark bruises around her eyes.

"No. He was trying to break in."

"Think he'll die?" She went on, "He asked for it, you know. You can shoot if someone's trying to break in, can't you? I wasn't trying to kill him."

I put a hand on her arm, and she didn't pull away. "I don't think he's going to die, and I think you were within your rights to shoot him, although it would have been better if you hadn't. He's pretty harmless."

She looked at my hand and then threw herself in my arms. "Shawn's going to have a sex change operation anyway. We're not going to have children."

I patted her on the back. "I'm sorry. I thought you were going to see him through it."

She sniffed. "I was."

"Are you?" I spoke soothingly as if she were a client.

"Do you think I should? What will it be like when he's a she? Will I want to have sex with her?"

187

These were questions she should have asked herself earlier, but I bit my tongue and continued to pat her back.

She drew away, dug around in the pocket of her robe for a tissue, and wiped her nose. "Want a cup of coffee?"

"Decaf would be okay." Sometime between now and Monday morning, I needed to sleep.

We sat on the porch and drank the decaf while the sky lightened. We were a little jumpy. Mona had her rifle by her side, which made me even more nervous.

When the birds began to sing, I slipped in next to Sally, whose steady breathing told me she still slept, even as she turned away from me. I felt as if my bones were melting from fatigue. Closing my eyes against the light that filtered into the room, I drifted into a welcome dream.

XXVIII

When I walked into the phone room for the staff meeting Monday morning, Debbie, Mark, and Bob were lined up on the couch—talking, drinking coffee, and eating doughnut holes. They looked at me as I sat in one of the chairs. The on-call person from the weekend hadn't shown up yet.

"Well, guess what," I began.

"You got another rabbit?" Mark said.

"That too. I wonder if it'll fool Mona," I said, momentarily distracted.

"Does it look like the other one?" Bob asked.

"It would fool me, except this one is litter box trained."

"That's a step forward."

"Something terrible happened Saturday," I blurted and launched into the story about Mona shooting Karl, which stunned them into uncharacteristic silence. "No comments?"

"I thought I'd heard everything, that I'd never be surprised again," Debbie said.

"Me, too," Bob admitted.

"Karl?" Mark questioned.

"Karl," I said firmly. "I'm on call today. Think I'll drop in on him at the hospital and find out what this was about. If he's up to it, that is. He never opened his eyes while he was lying on the ground Saturday night."

The person on call over the weekend walked in and sat down. She gave us the lowdown on the weekend and left. Before the four of us finished staffing, I was called to the hospital.

After taking care of the person in emergency, I went to Karl's room. He was pale but sitting up in bed. He looked startled to see me. There was no one in the other bed. He rubbed the grizzled stubbles on his chin and cheeks. "How'd you know I was here?" he asked.

"You were shot breaking into a house."

"I had no place to stay. There wasn't anybody there. I didn't take nothing." He looked away from me. "They didn't have no cause to shoot me."

"What would you do if someone was jimmying your lock in the middle of the night, if that someone had obviously been inside the house, sleeping in the beds?" I was suddenly indignant. "That was my house, Karl."

"You shot me?" His mouth opened in surprise.

"No, my sister did. I recognized you."

"I thought one of them pictures looked like you." Of course, there were photos of me. "I didn't know it was your house."

Whose house it was would come out in the trial or I wouldn't have told him. I didn't want my clients to know where I lived. "I thought your driver's license was revoked."

His gaze slid sideways. "How's a person supposed to get around?"

"The police towed your car. You're in real trouble now, Karl." Of course, he'd probably get a minor sentence and be out in a matter of weeks or months.

"C'mon Abby. I'm sorry. I paid for it. I nearly got killed. My side hurts like hell." The bullet had grazed his rib cage, cracking a couple on its way in and out. Nothing too serious.

"Yeah well, you were lucky. My sister's an expert shot. You would've been dead if she could have seen you." Disgusted with both of us—me for revealing too much, him for his whining—I turned and went out the door.

After work, I went to the humane association to pick up the rabbit. It was heavy in the kennel, and I set it in the back seat where it hopped in a tight circle before hunkering down, its pink nose twitching.

"Okay, Hops, you're on your way to a new home. Get your lucky foot out. We have to fool Mona." Mona might tell me she didn't want another rabbit if she couldn't have Hops, and I'd be stuck with the bunny.

Her car was in the garage. I peeked in the window as I carried Hops to the back door. Normally, we left the back door open during the day when we were home. I set the kennel down and dug in my purse for my key, hoping Mona wouldn't shoot me through the door. I pounded once on the panel and yelled her name before inserting the key.

The door swung open. Mona stood framed in it. She squatted to look in the kennel at the panting rabbit.

"Take her out," I said. "It's hot in there."

She gathered the rabbit in her arms, crooning, "It's bitsy bunny. Come to mama."

I picked up the empty kennel and walked inside behind her. She leaned on the counter for a moment with the rabbit in her arms, but the new Hops wanted down. She set her on the floor and the bunny made a beeline for the litter box.

"How'd you get her to do that?"

"I kept her in the kennel and let her out every few hours."

"I'm not going to keep her in that kennel. That's inhumane."

I shrugged. "Maybe."

191

"How's Karl?"

"Alive." I was surprised she remembered his name.

"I've got two painting jobs. One is on Wednesday after work. Another's on Saturday."

"No kidding," I said. "That's great."

"Yeah. I just started to advertise. Shawn is going to help. He says if I'm willing to be there for him, he'll be there for me. That's good, isn't it?" She answered her own question. "That's good."

"I've got groceries in the car. I'll get them." She followed me out, talking.

"Was Karl drunk? Did he really stay at the house last week? Why did he choose our house? Was it because you know him? Was his car towed?"

"Slow down, woman. Yes, he was staying here. Yes, they towed his car. Yes, he was drunk, but I don't think he knew it was my house. He does now, though." I handed her a bag and took one myself.

The sun homed in on my shoulders as I made my way inside. I loved summer, especially when it came on the heels of a long winter.

The rabbit was nowhere in sight. It had left a pile of perfectly round turds in the litter box. Mona set the bag down and began emptying it. I'd planned to make Chinese chicken salad, a cold dish.

We worked together. She talked about Shawn and his plans for the sex change operation. It was to take place locally when he was ready. She'd see him through it, nurse him back to health, and go from there. "Is that fair or what?" she asked and went on before I could answer. "I'll stick with him through the surgery, even if he's not doing what he said he'd do. We were going to have kids before he had surgery. Remember? He said we wouldn't be the best parents. He actually told me that at Sally's cabin. On our honeymoon."

"Sounds like he was being honest with you," I put in.

Shawn walked in then and she clammed up. He kissed her on

the cheek, said hello to both of us, and went upstairs to change. When he came down, wearing shorts and a baggy t-shirt, I noticed he had very little facial hair. I saw again that he'd be a beautiful woman. He was a gorgeous man.

When the chicken was cooked, I tore it up and put it on the Napa cabbage with green onions. Mixing the dressing, I poured it over the top. I'd bought a loaf of Italian bread to go with it. We ate on the sunporch with the glass doors thrown open. A hot, damp breeze flowed through the screens. Lightning flashed on the eastern horizon. The sun hovered above the trees surrounded by a yellow haze.

"It's gonna rain again," Shawn remarked. "Did I see a rabbit inside? I thought I saw something white."

"Where was she?" I asked.

"Behind the couch."

"I'll get her," Mona said.

"Leave her be." Shawn put in. "Maybe she wants to be alone."

But Mona got her anyway and brought her out to the porch where she huddled under the table, eating scraps of lettuce Mona fed her.

Shawn reached down, picked the animal up, and looked under her tail. I saw what he did—a small, empty pouch. This was a neutered male rabbit. Why hadn't I inquired about its sex? I met Shawn's eyes, saw the puzzlement, and lifted my brows.

Later that night he asked me about the rabbit, and I told him the truth. He said he'd pretend not to have noticed its sex. Maybe Mona never would.

Rain fell during the night and continued the next day, but there was no cooling in it. I splashed through puddles to Elizabeth's apartment. I'd promised to drop in to see how she and Anna were doing.

Anna refused to unlock the door when I gave her my name. "You're the one who locked me up in the hospital," she shouted.

We were back to base one. "Is Elizabeth there?" I asked, loud enough for my voice to travel beyond her.

"Who is it, Anna?" Elizabeth asked.

"No one," Anna snapped.

"Abby Dean," I yelled, feeling foolish.

Elizabeth opened the door to the length of chain, then unlatched it. "Come on in, Abby." I saw Anna's back disappearing into the hallway.

"How's it going?" The police in the squad car had checked me out.

Elizabeth lifted a shoulder. "As good as it gets. It's not much fun being watched all the time."

"Better them than Brume," I said.

"Can I get you anything? Coffee?"

"Sure. A cup of decaf would be nice."

She poured two cups and sat down with me.

"Have you heard from him?" I asked.

"No." She'd lost weight, and there were bags under her eyes.

"You look tired," I said.

"I don't sleep well. I go to work; I come home. They go with me when I grocery shop. It's not living. It's waiting for James to show up."

I wondered how long the police would watch over her. "Maybe he left town. If I were him, I would have."

"Yeah, well you're not him." She looked gloomily into her coffee cup.

I leaned forward and touched her shoulder. "Do you want to call off the police?"

A look of panic crossed her face. "No. I want to know why this one person manages to control everything I do?"

I said nothing. She knew the answer to the question. She'd given him the control. "Be careful who you trust." I spoke gently. Setting my coffee cup on the table, I asked, "How are you and Anna getting along?"

"She's so . . ."

"Not there?" I suggested.

"That's it." She looked at me expectantly.

"She's alone in her little world. Has she been hearing voices?"

"You're talking about me," Anna said accusingly, shuffling into the living room.

"We'd rather talk with you," I said.

"You're not going to put me away again." Fear flickered in her eyes.

"I'm leaving now. I'll stop by soon."

"Don't," Anna said.

"Do," Elizabeth urged. "Next week. I'm going nuts here."

I clattered down the stairs. Their flat was on the second floor. It made it harder to break into. The squad car was parked across the street.

The report came from behind me, shockingly loud, and something smashed into my leg, knocking it out from under me.

XXIX

Agonizing pain burned through my thigh. I grabbed it with both hands, and my fingers slid in wetness. I knew I ought to be running, instead of lying in full view on the sidewalk, but my leg wouldn't obey when I scrabbled to get up.

The police flew out of the squad car. One ran toward me, the other shot in the direction of the bullet that had disabled me. I gritted my teeth.

"Let's get you in the car." Scott McLane knelt at my side. He put an arm under my arms and dragged me to my feet. I screamed. The landscape tilted out of focus. Shots resounded around us, like we were in the center of a shoot-out. It was surreal, but sometimes so was the world I worked in.

Scott half dragged me toward the squad car. Determination of will over each step's burst of pain kept me moving. Elizabeth appeared on my other side, her pupils wide with fear. She took my arm. "It's my fault. I'm sorry," she said.

"Get back inside and lock your door. Are you nuts?" Scott snapped.

Elizabeth whimpered and disappeared. Scott shoved me in the front seat of the police car and jumped behind the wheel. He pulled away from the curb, leaving his partner behind. I lay back against the headrest and everything slid away.

Sally stood in the trout stream, dressed in one of her many suits. She cast and snagged me in the leg, then tried to reel me in like a fish. I yelled, but it made no difference. She kept saying, "I've got a really big one."

I twisted, trying to get off the hook. Hops swam by, and I reached for her. She bit me in the leg and turned into a beaver with huge, yellow teeth. "I didn't mean for her to die," I sobbed, swallowing water.

"Yes, you did." Mona now held the rod jerking my leg. Sally had disappeared.

I came to on a gurney in the emergency room, where I'd so often seen people while on call. The pain had subsided somewhat. I supposed they'd given me a shot of morphine. My leg was bandaged from the knee to groin.

"We're not used to seeing you as the patient." Carol Watkins smiled. She was taking my vitals.

I didn't recognize the doctor who entered the cubicle. His badge read David Chaffee, MD. "How's the pain, Ms. Dean?"

"Better." My mouth felt as if all the moisture had been sucked from it.

"The bullet passed through the thigh without hitting any bone. However, it damaged muscle. It'll be a while before you walk normally again. We're going to transfer you to a bed upstairs overnight."

I nodded.

"Abby's with the county crisis unit," Carol said. "We're not used to seeing her as a patient."

"Is getting shot part of your work?" Dr. Chaffee asked with a smile.

"It wasn't in my job description," I responded.

"I hope not. Take it easy now. Give that leg a chance to heal."

He patted me on the arm, the one without the needles and blood pressure cuff, and left.

"I think you need a drink of water," Carol said.

"I do," I croaked.

"Who should we notify?" she asked when she returned.

"Work," I said, and then gave her Sally's name and number, too.

I must have fallen asleep, because when I awoke I was in a bed near the window in a double room. An older woman peered at me from the other bed.

"What happened to your leg?" she asked.

"Somebody shot me," I replied, hoping she wouldn't believe me.

"A jealous boyfriend?" she inquired.

"No. I don't know who it was." I closed my eyes to shut out any more questions.

When I opened them again, Sally and Mona were on one side of the bed and Debbie, Mark, and Bob on the other.

"What are you all doing here?"

"Hiding. We might be next," Bob joked. Debbie socked him in the arm. "Oops. Not funny, I know. How do you feel?"

"Feels like somebody took a sledgehammer to my leg. Did they get him? Was it Brume?" I was having trouble staying awake, and squinted to keep them in focus.

Mona threw herself on the bed. "I'm gonna find this guy and kill him. Are you sure it wasn't Karl?"

Startled fully awake, I patted her hair. "I never saw him, and Karl was in the hospital."

"I'll get him. Don't worry. He won't shoot at my sister any-more." I almost reminded her that she'd shot at me. She glanced up at Debbie, Mark, and Bob across the narrow expanse of the white bed. "I'm a crack shot, you know."

"We know," Mark said, "but do you know what Brume looks like?"

Mona's blue eyes flooded with tears. She blinked a couple times to clear them. "I saw him on TV."

"Don't shoot anyone. Okay? You may be in trouble for shooting Karl. Promise me, Mona. I have to go to sleep, and I want your promise that you'll put your guns away." My words slurred and tumbled over each other.

Mona gave me a troubled look. "What if somebody breaks into the house again?"

"That's not going to happen," Sally said. "In Abby's present state, she can't be worrying about you. Give her your word, Mona."

"All right," Mona barked, again startling me out of a doze. "I won't touch my guns. I swear." She held up her right hand. "But I think it's a mistake. Abby needs someone to protect her. Can you do that? Any of you?" She looked at the others. "I didn't think so."

"The police will protect her," Debbie promised.

"Yeah, like they protected her today. Weren't they right there?"

I couldn't stay awake any longer. "Thanks for coming," I said, sounding as if I were drunk.

Their voices penetrated my shallow sleep. They talked over me—Mona rambling about revenge, Sally telling her to cool it, my three co-workers saying they'd be back tomorrow after work.

I peeked out of one eye and saw only Sally. "Mona's gone?" I asked.

She nodded. "She went home to see if Shawn's there. I suggested she wait till tomorrow to come back. How long are they keeping you?"

"Overnight, I think." I felt the morphine tugging me down a tunnel and swallowed nausea. "Maybe they could take me off this pain machine. It makes me want to puke."

"I'll ask."

She disappeared into the hallway and returned with a nurse, who, after checking with the hospital doctor, disconnected me from the machine.

When the nurse was gone, I asked Sally if they'd caught Brume. I thought she looked elegant in a light blue, linen suit.

"They didn't find him. They didn't even see his vehicle. They don't know if it was Brume."

"Who else would it be? Damn, I'm tired of that man." It's not like I was involved with him. My connection was peripheral and reluctant.

"Why don't you sleep?" she suggested. "I'll sit here for a while."

"You don't have to." But I wanted her to.

"I've got a briefcase full of work." She patted the fat leather bag by the side of her chair.

Darkness fell before I next awakened. The room was softly bathed in exterior lights from the parking lot. Even the lights in the hallway appeared dimmed. Footsteps occasionally hurried past the door in answer to buzzers. I wondered why I didn't have to pee, then saw the catheter going into a bag fastened to the rail of the bed.

The lady in the next bed had left while I slept. I was glad not to have to answer any more unwanted questions.

My leg throbbed with every pulse of blood. I tried another position and clenched my teeth not to cry out. Pushing the call button, I waited impatiently for the nurse to appear at my bedside.

When she did, she took my blood pressure and my pulse. "Time for a vitals check anyway."

"Can I have something for the pain?"

"Sure. Your vital signs are stable. I'll be right back."

The rattling of the food cart in the hallway brought me around next. Daylight took away the disorienting shadows of the night. An aide brought me a breakfast tray. I peeked under the lids at warm oatmeal, toasted white bread, a poached egg, with coffee, juice, and a small bowl of prunes.

I'd been shot before eating dinner and didn't realize how hungry I was until I took a mouthful. Devouring everything on the tray, I fell back on the pillows and waited for someone to dismiss me.

Shortly after my tray was taken away, my family doctor, John Singleton, stepped into the room. He was tall with thick black hair, dark eyes, and a mostly gray mustache. I liked him. We usually talked politics.

"You're up early," I said with some surprise at his appearance, although I knew family doctors were always notified when their patients were hospitalized.

"How's the leg?" He pulled on gloves and began to unwrap the bandage.

"It hurts." I watched nervously, noticing that as he removed the pressure, the pain became more intense. Nevertheless, I wanted to see the wound.

"I've been told it feels like you've been hit by a baseball bat, then probed by a hot poker."

"That's a good description," I said, sucking in air.

The leg was severely bruised around the blackened edges of the hole. It looked as bad as it felt. Singleton put some antibiotic on the wound and fresh gauze pads, then rewrapped the leg.

"You're going to have to keep your weight off that for a while. We'll get you some crutches. How did this happen?"

"It wasn't on the news?"

"I didn't see the news."

"Someone shot me as I left a client's apartment, possibly the guy who escaped from the county jail, who held the same client hostage a few weeks ago. He shot her then."

"Maybe you should take a leave of absence." He looked at me intently. Long black hairs grew out of his unruly eyebrows. "This country bristles with guns."

"My sister shot someone breaking into our home. It turned out to be one of my clients, although I don't think he knew it was my home."

"I read about that." Mona was his patient, too. "How is Mona?"

"A little manic, as always."

He smiled and nodded, his eyes warm. "You need to take care of yourself, Abby. Don't worry about Mona. Don't worry about work. I'd like to keep you here another day."

"Okay," I said meekly.

He squeezed my arm and was gone.

I phoned Sally. It was just after six in the morning. She would still be in bed.

"Did I wake you?"

"Nope. I was just getting ready to get up. How are you feeling?"

"Dr. Singleton just left. He rewrapped the wound. It looks pretty bad. He wants to keep me here another day. Can you bring my book?"

"Sure. I'll be there at noon. I've got court in the morning."

XXX

I recovered at Sally's. In a few days I'd read everything in sight and was restlessly swinging my way around the house on my crutches.

It gave me time to think. If I were Brume, I'd be long gone from the area. However, I'd dealt with abusive clients too long to be fooled into such thinking. Revenge figured high in their scheme of things. They always managed to convince themselves that they were the victims, no matter what they did.

I called Elizabeth on Friday, not knowing her working hours, and Anna answered. "Who is this?" she asked suspiciously.

I told her. "How are you, Anna?"

"I don't have time to talk. I'm going to the store. I have to sneak past those cops out there, or they'll put me away."

That was a long speech for Anna. "No they won't, Anna. They'll take you to the store."

"They're always telling me what to do, just like you. Go away.

Leave me alone." I wasn't sure if she was talking to me or to one of her voices.

"Tell Elizabeth to call Abby. Please?" I started to give her Sally's number, but she hung up.

I rang the police department and asked for Scott McLane. He came on the line after a few moments.

"Hi, Scott. This is Abby Dean."

"Where are you? Are you all right?"

"Yes, I'm fine. I'm staying with a friend, Sally Shields. She's an attorney."

"I know her. Listen, I'm sorry. You shouldn't have been shot."

"It wasn't your fault. I'm calling about something else, though." I told him I was worried about Anna leaving the safety of the apartment. "I thought maybe you could alert the guys in the squad car. Would you give me a callback about this?"

An hour passed, during which I sat on the porch staring out the window with a book on my lap. I was pacing again when he called. There was a lot of noise in the background.

"Abby, I'm at the apartment now. Well, first of all, I want you to know that Anna and Elizabeth are all right. The police followed Anna to the store and back, because she wouldn't get into the car with them. While they were gone, though, James Brume got into the apartment and was waiting when Elizabeth got home from work."

"Are you sure she's all right?" I asked anxiously. I'd called off the cops, Elizabeth's only protection. Where were my brains? Brume was after Elizabeth, not Anna.

"A little traumatized. They took her to the hospital." He paused. "Is Mona Lawrence your sister?"

"Yes." My heart took the well-known plunge. What had Mona done now?

"She apparently staked out the apartment. When she saw Brume go into the building, she hid behind a tree until he came out, holding Elizabeth at gunpoint. As near as we can tell, she stepped out from behind the tree and shot him in the head."

"What?" But I knew it was true. I felt nauseous. Only the crutches held me up.

"She didn't run. She walked over to make sure he was dead. She must be a crack shot."

"She is," I said dully, my heart racing. I always knew Mona would do something irretrievably awful when I wasn't watching. "Where is she?"

"At the police station."

No wonder Elizabeth was traumatized. She'd been splattered with brains and blood, I learned later. She'd screamed until the police led her away.

"Thanks for calling, Scott."

"I'm sorry it happened this way," he said.

After he hung up, I stood holding the receiver, listening to the dial tone while the implications of my phone call to the police about Anna sunk in. As soon as I hung up Shawn called.

"I know," I said as he started to tell me. "The police called."

"Sally's with her right now. Are you coming down? She keeps saying she did it for you." He sounded angry.

"She probably thought she did. I'll be there soon."

My initial shock was slowly turning to anger and concern. I'd heard and believed it true that once someone killed another person, they overcame much of the taboo that went with it. It became easier to kill again. Having shot Karl might have paved the way for this shooting.

I couldn't stay in the house any longer while Mona was locked up. I had to see her and talk to Sally. Throwing my crutches and purse in the backseat, I pulled myself behind the wheel of the Saturn. Grunting with pain, I lifted my injured left leg and dragged it in with me. The car had been shut up for days and the interior was sweltering. I started the engine, turned on the air, and pressed the button to unroll the windows.

At the jail I managed to extract myself from the car and swing my way inside. "Don't I know you?" the young woman behind the desk asked.

"I'm Abby Dean. You were here when I came to see James Brume. Now I'm here to see Mona Lawrence."

"She's with her attorney and husband. They're in the first room down the hall toward the cells. I need to see some ID, though," she said apologetically.

I showed her my county ID badge, and she waived me on. "Go ahead. I'll tell them you're coming."

Shawn opened the door before I got there. Crutches slowed me down considerably. "How is she?" I asked in low tones.

He shrugged. He wore his work clothes—overalls and a T-shirt. His tousled hair hung halfway down his neck. It was going to be hard to call him Shirley again.

Mona and Sally faced each other across a table. Sally smiled distractedly. "Just give me a few minutes alone with Mona. Okay? I won't take long."

I turned around and went back into the hall with Shawn, who sighed when we sat on a bench outside the door. "What?" I asked.

He shook his head and leaned against the wall. "I don't know what to think."

On the one hand, Mona had saved Elizabeth's life. On the other, she was beginning to look like someone who didn't value life. "Neither do I. Think we can get those guns away from her?"

"She'll just replace them. How can I stay, knowing she might shoot me if I surprise her or if she gets mad enough?"

"Are you looking for a reason to leave?"

"Maybe," he admitted. "It's not going well since I decided we shouldn't have kids and told her I wanted to go ahead with the sex change. She doesn't let me sleep. She talks all the time."

"It's part of the bipolar disorder."

"I suppose she'll have to put up bail."

"I expect." My leg throbbed under the bandages. It felt best when it was on the same level as my heart.

Shawn nodded toward the front desk. Dennis stood there, looking our way. He came over and thumped down beside me. I'd last seen him when he and Nance had visited me my second night in the hospital. He smelled of fresh air.

"Mona shot that guy dead, huh?" he said.

I nodded.

"Well, good riddance," he added. "He tried to kill you."

There were no witnesses to my shooting, but maybe someone would come forward now that Brume was dead. "Whoever shot me had very bad aim."

Dennis patted my hand. "Thank God."

The door opened, and Sally let us in to see a tearful Mona. Before she was taken to a cell, I gave her a hug and told her to be brave.

"I did it for you," she said.

"Shh. Don't admit to anything. Talk to Sally first." She was my little sister. I loved her. It occurred to me she could always plead not guilty by reason of insanity.

Sally walked out with me as Dennis and Shawn drove off. "Should you be behind a wheel?"

"I couldn't stay at your house after I heard." I made my way to my car, where Sally waited while I got myself inside.

"I'll be home around six," she said, heading toward her BMW. "I'll pick up a pizza."

I thought I wouldn't be hungry, but I was. Using crutches not only slowed me down, but took more energy. I was losing weight.

Over the pizza, Sally said, "I think we'll risk a guilty plea. If we don't get a plea bargain, the jury will be sympathetic. You'll have to testify."

"It was my fault, you know."

She looked at me with interest, her dark eyes puzzled. "You pulled the trigger?"

"I asked the police to follow Anna. That's how Brume got into Elizabeth's apartment."

"You did what you thought was best. In the end, Mona's responsible for her own actions."

If it were only that easy, I thought, knowing I would always feel partly responsible.

I went with Shawn and Sally the next day to put up bond for Mona's release. After, the four of us stood outside the courthouse, three of us worrying about leaving Mona alone.

"I'll take you to your car, Mona," Shawn said, "but then I have to go to work."

"Are you going home?" Sally asked Mona.

"I have to wash the jail off me," Mona said. "Do you want me to come to work?"

"Not today."

"You've got a lot of jobs to call back about," Shawn said. "That'll keep you busy." I knew the wall painting business was prospering and wondered if people would become wary now that Mona had killed Brume.

I offered to follow Mona home and stay with her. The old fire lit up her eyes.

"I don't need another guard," she snapped.

So I went to work. I figured it would take me the rest of the day to catch up on my e-mail, and the building was next to the courthouse. Debbie, Mark, and Bob had carried on without me cheerfully. My boss had told me to take as much time as I needed, but I was bored and too worried about Mona to stay idle any longer.

Debbie carried coffee for me to my office. "Couldn't stay away, huh?" She set the cup on my desk as Mark and Bob popped their heads into the room.

"You knew we couldn't get along without you," Bob said.

"How's Mona?" Mark asked the question for them.

"Out on bail. I hope she went home." I smiled grimly. "You know all about it, I suppose?"

They nodded. "Sorry," Mark said for all of them.

"No one's going to convict her," Debbie added.

Sylvia appeared between the two men. "I hope you're not coming back too early," she said.

"I just thought I'd catch up on my e-mail," I said. "I was over at the courthouse." Their concern made me want to cry.

"We'll leave you to it then," Sylvia said.

I went home to Sally, hoping nothing had gone awry in my absence. Mona's line had been busy whenever I called that afternoon. I tried again at Sally's, and Mona answered.

"How's it going?" I asked.

"I've got more jobs than I can handle," she said cheerfully, as if everything were normal. "Shawn and I'll have to work nights and Saturday."

"Want me to come out and see you Sunday?" I wasn't surprised that she hadn't thanked me for putting up half the bail. She no doubt thought she'd done me a favor by shooting Brume.

"Give a call first," she replied.

"Is Shawn home?"

"Not yet. I've got to go now."

The next day Elizabeth showed up for the appointment that had been set before Brume's death. Her eyes were sunken, the skin around them discolored by lack of sleep. I knew they had treated her in the emergency room and sent her home. I should have called, but I hadn't.

She squeezed her purse convulsively as she talked with shudders about the warm blood splattering her, of the back of Brume's head being blown away. She spoke in low tones about the terror of finding him in her apartment with a gun. How she'd thought she was going to die, and then how she'd thought she had when Mona's gun went off at such close range.

"I'm terribly sorry," I said. "I feel responsible for all this."

Her haunted gaze was one I could hardly meet. "Why?"

"Mona's my sister. She thought Brume shot me. That's why she was there. I think she believed she was saving you, though."

"She did. It's just that it was too much at once. You know?"

I did know. I could only listen and try to comfort her. Before she left I asked how Anna was.

"The same, and that's a comfort." She smiled. "Guess what her only comment was?"

"That when she hit Brume over the head she should have killed him," I said.

"You got it. See you next week?"

"You bet." I showed her out. She was my only client that day. The rest I'd canceled.

Sally and I drove to her cabin for the Fourth of July weekend. We stopped first at the Duck Crossing to see Ted. As I swung myself into the bar, he boomed, "Somebody shoot you?"

"Yep," I replied, sliding my bottom onto a barstool. My leg throbbed, and I put the toe of my shoe on the foot rail to take the weight off it. I knew he wouldn't believe me.

Sally smiled and ordered for both of us. "Anything new?" she asked.

"Jerry Whitlock, your neighbor, caught a twenty-inch trout just down the stream from you. Then he had a stroke and nearly drowned."

"No kidding," I said, feeling a spurt of sympathy. He wouldn't be showing up unexpectedly at our door, though. We'd have some privacy, I thought with a little accompanying guilt.

"Poor guy. I'll be next." He patted his immense belly, and I thought he probably would.

That night we lay in a single bed with all the windows open and listened to silence. No lights, no fireworks, no cars, no one but us talking. A light breeze blew hot air through the screens. We had to either lie on our backs with our sides touching or lie back to front, spoon style. I draped an arm over Sally's waist and fell asleep but woke later in a sweat and moved to another bed where there was more room for my wounded leg.

Considering I could neither hike nor fish nor even get down to the water, the weekend passed with amazing speed. I was pretty much confined to sitting with a book in the fickle sunlight in front of the cabin overlooking the stream. We made careful love a couple of times. At night we played Scrabble and cribbage and read.

On Sunday as we were getting ready to leave, Sally asked, "Have you given any more thought to living here after what happened?"

I couldn't afford to retire. "I never thought of my job as risky. I suppose no one does until some disgruntled employee or client pulls a gun." I shrugged a shoulder. "It could happen to anyone, and it could happen here."

She looked up from the cooler with a wry smile. "Some client unhappy over a will could do me in, I suppose."

"Hey, money is what drives people."

She tossed the local newspaper in my direction. It was folded back to the classified section. "The county's hiring in mental health. They're looking for a supervisor."

I glanced at the ad she'd been serious enough to circle. "What would you do? Open an office here?"

"I'd commute when I had to. I'd solicit work here, too."

Maybe I'd been in one place too long. I was comfortable there, though. My co-workers were my friends. Clients like Elizabeth needed me. "I guess I'm not ready for a change yet. It's a little isolated here. I'm pretty sure I'd be lonely. There are no movie theaters or stores close by. Not even a video place. Think of the new performing arts center. Wouldn't you hate to give up the opportunity to go there?"

There was also the problem of Mona. If Shawn left her, she'd be dumped in my lap, that is if she wasn't under lock and key. A shiver passed through me. Sally and I hadn't talked much about Mona's fate. I inserted her into the conversation. "I don't think Mona would do well in prison."

Sally put the lid on the cooler, stood up, and tucked her hair behind her ears. "I don't think you have to worry about that."

"I am worried. She was nuts after one night in jail."

"I think you should worry more about whether Shawn leaves

her. Then what will you do, move back in?" She put her hands in the back pockets of her shorts in a sexy pose.

I looked away. "Well, I'll have to spend part of my time there anyway. You know that. Besides, the house is my responsibility, too," I said defensively. "You should spend time there with me."

Her mouth quirked a little in amusement. "On principle, I suppose."

"Yes." I smiled, glad to have avoided a confrontation.

"Ready to go?" she asked, looking around the interior of the cabin. Everything was in order. "Need some help?"

I put the crutches under my arms, picked up my backpack with one hand and my weekend bag with the other. "I carried them in, I can carry them out."

XXXI

Mona's trial started mid-October, when the landscape was painted with reds and golds. The day it began dawned sunny and warm. I'd taken vacation days to attend. It was the same courtroom where I'd been called to testify against Karl, who had been sentenced to six months of jail time followed by two years of parole. Gaunt, ashen, and shaky, he'd hung his head and responded meekly to the judge's questions.

The seats filled quickly, which surprised me since it was a weekday. I sat behind Mona and Sally, who were on the other side of the railing separating the onlookers from the participants. Shawn held a space for me till I got there.

He wore slacks and a nice shirt, sort of a unisex outfit. His wavy blond hair shone under the fluorescent lights. People threw curious glances at him or stared outright. He slid over to make room and whispered in my ear, "Mona's crazy with worry."

Mona turned and gave me a sickly smile, which I returned. "Hang in there," I mouthed. "It'll be all right."

Sally swiveled enough to catch my eye, and gave me a strained smile. That morning before we went our separate ways, she admitted she got a little uptight before a trial. Don was there by her side at Sally's insistence.

When Nance and Dennis came down the aisle, Shawn and I made room to squeeze them in. We rearranged ourselves so that Nance and I sat between Shawn and Dennis. Again, Mona turned. Nance gave her both thumbs up.

Feet shuffling, we all stood when Judge Neff entered from the judge's chambers. He sat behind the imposing wooden dais and we settled back into our seats. The court was called to order, and the attorneys gave their opening statements. Jury selection had taken place the two previous days, during which I opted to work.

The prosecuting attorney, Ed Banks, said Mona was trigger happy. First shooting Karl Jankowski through a closed and locked door. Then tracking Brume down in order to shoot him. She killed Brume not in self-defense, he said, but as an act of vengeance. It was only happenstance that Elizabeth got away and luck that she hadn't been killed instead.

I was impressed with Sally, by her composed stance, slightly spread-legged, hands in suit jacket pockets. She told the jury that Mona was defending her sister, who had been shot by Brume. A witness had come forward, a neighboring woman who, as it turned out, called the police to report seeing him there.

Sally pointed out that Brume had earlier held Elizabeth hostage and shot her. When released on bail, he broke into Providence House and re-injured Elizabeth. After being jailed again, he escaped, shot a policeman who was guarding Elizabeth, and later shot me as I left Elizabeth's apartment. He had broken into Elizabeth's apartment and forced her outside at gunpoint when Mona shot him, thus saving Elizabeth.

I leaned forward. Nance gave my hand a squeeze. My back and neck ached with tension. Perhaps Sally had made a mistake, not using an insanity defense. Whom would I believe, I asked myself. Both, probably.

Two policemen described finding Brume shot dead with Mona standing over him and Elizabeth screaming hysterically nearby. The prosecution called Karl Jankowski as a witness. Karl wore an orange jumpsuit, which made his shoulders look like a clothes hanger. His skin was gray from sickliness or lack of sunlight. He answered questions in a low voice.

"I heard the shot and seen it blow a hole in the door before it hit me. I went down right away. Jesus, I just needed a place to sleep."

"Did anyone ask who was at the door before shooting you?"

"I don't think so."

Sally came on strong. "You were trying to get into someone else's house in the middle of the night. Someone you didn't know. That's called breaking and entering. Do you recognize Mona Lawrence, the defendant?"

"Nope. Like I said, I never saw her."

Sarcasm edged into Sally's voice. "How did you happen to choose her house to use as a free motel?"

"No one was there. No car in the garage. I damn near died from loss of blood."

"How long had you been living in Mona Lawrence's home before she returned to it?"

"Only a couple of days," Karl said sullenly. "I should've looked in the garage that night."

"What would you do if someone was breaking into your house in the wee hours of the morning?"

"I wouldn't have hurt her."

"She didn't know that, did she?"

Elizabeth Halbertson took the stand for the defense. Her voice shook as she spoke of the terror she felt, when Brume held her hostage last March and when she came home in July to find the police protection gone and James Brume waiting with a gun in her apartment. She thought she was going to die both times, she said. Brume was violent.

Banks asked her if Mona said anything to Brume before shooting him. Did she give him any warning? In a quiet voice Elizabeth said she didn't remember. She was too scared.

Jane Dougherty testified to Brume's breaking into Providence House. She told how the residents had beaten him into unconsciousness. The police corroborated her testimony. A titter passed through the audience.

When I took the stand, I was nervous. I often testified when clients needed to be detained. This was the first time my sister had been charged with a crime, though, the first time someone I loved was in jeopardy. I talked about my dealings with Brume. Banks asked if I told Mona that Brume had shot me. I couldn't honestly recall, but that was the general assumption being made, seeing that I was outside Elizabeth's apartment at the time.

Surprisingly, Mona kept her mouth shut as Sally had instructed her. I only had to look at her squirming in her chair to know how much she wanted to testify.

When it was all over, the jury found Mona guilty of aggravated assault. The judge put her on parole for one year and revoked her license to own a gun. Mona looked stunned. She accepted a hug from Sally, then turned and fell into Shawn's arms. Shawn lifted her over the railing separating them.

Relief washed over me, leaving me weak-kneed. Nance propped me up with a hug. Dennis shook Shawn's hand and patted Mona's shoulder. Nance squeezed both their arms, then she and Dennis left.

Sally was quietly jubilant. She shook hands with Don, who grabbed his briefcase and started up the aisle. The public defender took her hand and leaned forward to say something before following Don into the exiting crowd.

I asked her what Banks said, after we were seated at a table in the wine bar, where I was treating her to a victory dinner.

"He told me Mona did everyone a favor when she killed Brume." She smiled a little. "It would have made him unpopular to put Mona away. She's something of a folk heroine around town. Did you know that?"

I didn't. It would fit Mona's picture of herself when she was grandiose. At least, I wouldn't be making prison visits unless they were work-related. Sally had saved me from that.

We drove out to the house the next night to have dinner with Shawn and Mona. Night had fallen already. I wasn't looking forward to winter, to waking and going home in darkness as if the day belonged only to work. I said so.

"I've been thinking we should go somewhere warm in February," Sally suggested.

"Like where? Arizona to see my folks?"

"We could do that. Take a long weekend. Your mom and dad invited me. We could also go for a week to Mexico or the Caribbean or Hawaii."

"Let's," I said.

The bunny met us at the door. Mona had yet to notice that the new Hops was a he not a she. She did remark more than once that Hops had cleaned up her act while she and Shawn were on their honeymoon. To that I said I couldn't let her crap all over Sally's house.

I picked the bunny up and ran a hand over his soft fur. Neither Shawn nor Mona were in the kitchen, and I walked through the house to my bedroom, leaving Sally on the davenport reading the newspaper. I wanted to see the naked ladies. Hearing Shawn and Mona's voices behind their bedroom door, I flopped on my bed with the door open.

When Shawn emerged, freshly showered and dressed in slacks and a polo shirt, he rapped on the doorframe.

"Where's your other half?"

"Downstairs. How's Mona?"

"She was up all night. Talking."

"I suppose."

"We came to a resolution."

"And what was that?"

"If she lets me sleep, I'll stay." He winked. "I've got to get the hors d'oeuvres out. What do you want to drink?"

"We're having drinks?"

"That's part of the bargain. She doesn't drink, and she takes her meds."

"What's your part?"

"Be a good partner."

I didn't ask what that meant. He disappeared, and Mona took his place.

"Hey, sis. Did Sally tell you the news?"

"I was at the trial."

"Not that news. I quit the law firm. I've got enough painting jobs to keep me busy through the winter."

"Really?"

She took the bunny out of my arms and cuddled him. "Really. I'm a success. I've got my own business. What do you think of that?"

"Congratulations. Then we have two things to celebrate tonight."

"Don't you ever get excited, Abby? I think you could win the lottery and still wouldn't act any different. Are you coming downstairs or are you going to lie here?" She followed my gaze to the ladies. "Want me to repaint?"

"No. Leave my room alone. I like the ladies." I'd never told her that.

She grinned. "Okay, okay." And left me there.

I wanted to tell Mona that I was glad for her, but not excited over her recent business success, which could vanish anytime. I felt even happier for her, along with vast relief, over the result of the trial. What did excite me, I realized, was the possibility of finally having a life of my own with someone who wasn't my sister. Sally.

Mona yelled for me to come downstairs, saying that they would be on the sunporch. I went, reluctantly. Shawn handed me a vodka and tonic and raised his glass.

"To Sally," he toasted.

"To justice," Sally said.

"Hey, what about me?" Mona asked.

"To all of that and Mona's new business success," I put in, and we drank.

I popped a Mexican roll-up in my mouth and sipped the cold drink. Leaves whispered in the slight breeze.

"You should have put me on the stand, Sally," Mona said.

"Let it go, Mona," Shawn warned.

"But I had to kill him. He would have shot Elizabeth or me or both of us. He had the gun to her head." She turned to me. "Will you take the rifle Daddy gave me, Abby? I don't want to turn it in. I might not get it back."

"You didn't have to be there," I pointed out. "You shouldn't have been there."

"Then Elizabeth would be dead meat."

"Maybe, maybe not."

"I thought you turned in all your guns," Sally said.

"All but that one. My first rifle."

"For chrissake, Mona," I blurted. "A gun's a weapon, not something to get sentimental over."

"Will you keep it for me, though? Please?"

"I will if you tell me something," I said, knowing her persistence would wear me down.

"What?" she asked.

"What is it like to kill someone?"

"I felt worse killing a deer than shooting Brume." She looked away.

I didn't believe her. The taboo against murder was too great. "Could you have shot Brume if you hadn't shot Karl Jankowski?"

"Sure." She lifted a shoulder as if it was no big deal.

"I know police who need counseling after killing someone in the line of duty." I was watching her reactions more than heeding her words.

She met my eyes briefly, angrily. "Okay. I see them both at night when I can't sleep. All that blood, Elizabeth screaming, him looking surprised. I was just going to scare him, but he left me no choice."

I supposed she had to believe that. "Where's the rifle?"

"I'll get it."

When she handed it to me, I took it outside and put it in the BMW's trunk. Sally walked out with me. We stood in the driveway, looking at the stars and the harvest moon. A dusty, nutty smell hung in the air, one I associated with fall.

Sally took my hand and squeezed it. The touch set off a surge of happiness in me. I leaned against the BMW, thinking this was enough. She would keep me sane in all the madness. Maybe I could do the same for her.

Mona called, "Dinner's about ready."

"Come on, girlfriend," Sally said with a slight tug.

It occurred to me then that I associated passion with Mona's grandiosity. All these years I'd acted as a counterbalance to her mania and her depressions, reacting to her excesses by remaining rational. That way I at least controlled my environment. I doubted I would ever be free of the cautiousness her highs and lows inspired. Was that so bad?

"What are you thinking?" Sally asked as we walked toward the sunporch.

"Am I too low key?"

"You're a good foil for my thoughts. You're responsible, dependable, smart, pretty, and good in bed. It's everything I want."

"I could say the same about you, you know."

"Don't," she said. "It's like professing love after the other person does. Tell me some other time." We paused at the corner of the garage. "One Mona is enough."

"Don't I know it." I laughed. "I do love you, you know."

"I hope so. We shouldn't be doing what we're doing if you don't."

"Come on. Let's go see what they've cooked up for dinner."

Was Sally my passion? I put an arm around her, and the weight of Lisa's lingering question slid off me. Passion comes in degrees, doesn't it?

About the Author

Jackie Calhoun is the author of *Woman in the Mirror, Outside the Flock, Tamarack Creek,* and *Off Season,* published by Bella Books; ten romances published by Naiad Press; and *Crossing the Center Line,* printed by Windstorm Creative Ltd. Calhoun lives in northeastern Wisconsin.

LOVE SPEAKS HER NAME by Laura DeHart Young. 170 pp. Love and friendship, desire and intrigue, spark this exciting sequel to *Forever and the Night*.

ISBN 1-59493-002-3 $12.95

TO HAVE AND TO HOLD by Peggy J. Herring. 184 pp. By finally letting down her defenses, will Dorian be opening herself to a devastating betrayal?

ISBN 1-59493-005-8 $12.95

WILD THINGS by Karin Kallmaker. 228 pp. Dutiful daughter Faith has met the perfect man. There's just one problem: she's in love with his sister.   ISBN 1-931513-64-3 $12.95

SHARED WINDS by Kenna White. 216 pp. Can Emma rebuild more than just Lanny's marina?   ISBN 1-59493-006-6 $12.95

THE UNKNOWN MILE by Jaime Clevenger. 253 pp. Kelly's world is getting more and more complicated every moment.   ISBN 1-931513-57-0 $12.95

TREASURED PAST by Linda Hill. 189 pp. A shared passion for antiques leads to love.

ISBN 1-59493-003-1 $12.95

SIERRA CITY by Gerri Hill. 284 pp. Chris and Jesse cannot deny their growing attraction . . .   ISBN 1-931513-98-8 $12.95

ALL THE WRONG PLACES by Karin Kallmaker. 174 pp. Sex and the single girl—Brandy is looking for love and usually she finds it. Karin Kallmaker's first *After Dark* erotic novel.

ISBN 1-931513-76-7 $12.95

WHEN THE CORPSE LIES A Motor City Thriller by Therese Szymanski. 328 pp. Butch bad-girl Brett Higgins is used to waking up next to beautiful women she hardly knows. Problem is, this one's dead.   ISBN 1-931513-74-0 $12.95

GUARDED HEARTS by Hannah Rickard. 240 pp. Someone's reminding Alyssa about her secret past, and then she becomes the suspect in a series of burglaries.

ISBN 1-931513-99-6 $12.95

ONCE MORE WITH FEELING by Peggy J. Herring. 184 pp. Lighthearted, loving, romantic adventure.   ISBN 1-931513-60-0 $12.95

TANGLED AND DARK A Brenda Strange Mystery by Patty G. Henderson. 240 pp. When investigating a local death, Brenda finds two possible killers—one diagnosed with Multiple Personality Disorder.   ISBN 1-931513-75-9 $12.95

WHITE LACE AND PROMISES by Peggy J. Herring. 240 pp. Maxine and Betina realize sex may not be the most important thing in their lives.   ISBN 1-931513-73-2 $12.95

UNFORGETTABLE by Karin Kallmaker. 288 pp. Can Rett find love with the cheerleader who broke her heart so many years ago?   ISBN 1-931513-63-5 $12.95

HIGHER GROUND by Saxon Bennett. 280 pp. A delightfully complex reflection of the successful, high society lives of a small group of women.   ISBN 1-931513-69-4 $12.95

LAST CALL A Detective Franco Mystery by Baxter Clare. 240 pp. Frank overlooks all else to try to solve a cold case of two murdered children . . .   ISBN 1-931513-70-8 $12.95

ONCE UPON A DYKE: NEW EXPLOITS OF FAIRY-TALE LESBIANS by Karin Kallmaker, Julia Watts, Barbara Johnson & Therese Szymanski. 320 pp. You've never read fairy tales like these before! From Bella After Dark.   ISBN 1-931513-71-6 $14.95

FINEST KIND OF LOVE by Diana Tremain Braund. 224 pp. Can Molly and Carolyn stop clashing long enough to see beyond their differences?   ISBN 1-931513-68-6 $12.95

DREAM LOVER by Lyn Denison. 188 pp. A soft, sensuous, romantic fantasy.
ISBN 1-931513-96-1 $12.95

NEVER SAY NEVER by Linda Hill. 224 pp. A classic love story . . . where rules aren't the only things broken.
ISBN 1-931513-67-8 $12.95

PAINTED MOON by Karin Kallmaker. 214 pp. Stranded together in a snowbound cabin, Jackie and Leah's lives will never be the same.
ISBN 1-931513-53-8 $12.95

WIZARD OF ISIS by Jean Stewart. 240 pp. Fifth in the exciting Isis series.
ISBN 1-931513-71-4 $12.95

WOMAN IN THE MIRROR by Jackie Calhoun. 216 pp. Josey learns to love again, while her niece is learning to love women for the first time.
ISBN 1-931513-78-3 $12.95

SUBSTITUTE FOR LOVE by Karin Kallmaker. 200 pp. When Holly and Reyna meet the combination adds up to pure passion. But what about tomorrow?
ISBN 1-931513-62-7 $12.95

GULF BREEZE by Gerri Hill. 288 pp. Could Carly really be the woman Pat has always been searching for?
ISBN 1-931513-97-X $12.95

THE TOMSTOWN INCIDENT by Penny Hayes. 184 pp. Caught between two worlds, Eloise must make a decision that will change her life forever.
ISBN 1-931513-56-2 $12.95

MAKING UP FOR LOST TIME by Karin Kallmaker. 240 pp. Discover delicious recipes for romance by the undisputed mistress.
ISBN 1-931513-61-9 $12.95

THE WAY LIFE SHOULD BE by Diana Tremain Braund. 173 pp. With which woman will Jennifer find the true meaning of love?
ISBN 1-931513-66-X $12.95

BACK TO BASICS: A BUTCH/FEMME ANTHOLOGY edited by Therese Szymanski—from Bella After Dark. 324 pp.
ISBN 1-931513-35-X $14.95

SURVIVAL OF LOVE by Frankie J. Jones. 236 pp. What will Jody do when she falls in love with her best friend's daughter?
ISBN 1-931513-55-4 $12.95

LESSONS IN MURDER by Claire McNab. 184 pp. 1st Detective Inspector Carol Ashton Mystery.
ISBN 1-931513-65-1 $12.95

DEATH BY DEATH by Claire McNab. 167 pp. 5th Denise Cleever Thriller.
ISBN 1-931513-34-1 $12.95

CAUGHT IN THE NET by Jessica Thomas. 188 pp. A wickedly observant story of mystery, danger, and love in Provincetown.
ISBN 1-931513-54-6 $12.95

DREAMS FOUND by Lyn Denison. Australian Riley embarks on a journey to meet her birth mother . . . and gains not just a family, but the love of her life.
ISBN 1-931513-58-9 $12.95

A MOMENT'S INDISCRETION by Peggy J. Herring. 154 pp. Jackie is torn between her better judgment and the overwhelming attraction she feels for Valerie.
ISBN 1-931513-59-7 $12.95

IN EVERY PORT by Karin Kallmaker. 224 pp. Jessica has a woman in every port. Will meeting Cat change all that?
ISBN 1-931513-36-8 $12.95

TOUCHWOOD by Karin Kallmaker. 240 pp. Rayann loves Louisa. Louisa loves Rayann. Can the decades between their ages keep them apart?
ISBN 1-931513-37-6 $12.95

WATERMARK by Karin Kallmaker. 248 pp. Teresa wants a future with a woman whose heart has been frozen by loss. Sequel to *Touchwood*.
ISBN 1-931513-38-4 $12.95

EMBRACE IN MOTION by Karin Kallmaker. 240 pp. Has Sarah found lust or love?
ISBN 1-931513-39-2 $12.95

ONE DEGREE OF SEPARATION by Karin Kallmaker. 232 pp. Sizzling small town romance between Marian, the town librarian, and the new girl from the big city.
ISBN 1-931513-30-9 $12.95

CRY HAVOC A Detective Franco Mystery by Baxter Clare. 240 pp. A dead hustler with a headless rooster in his lap sends Lt. L.A. Franco headfirst against Mother Love.
ISBN 1-931513931-7 $12.95

DISTANT THUNDER by Peggy J. Herring. 294 pp. Bankrobbing drifter Cordy awakens strange new feelings in Leo in this romantic tale set in the Old West.
ISBN 1-931513-28-7 $12.95

COP OUT by Claire McNab. 216 pp. 4th Detective Inspector Carol Ashton Mystery.
ISBN 1-931513-29-5 $12.95

BLOOD LINK by Claire McNab. 159 pp. 15th Detective Inspector Carol Ashton Mystery. Is Carol unwittingly playing into a deadly plan? ISBN 1-931513-27-9 $12.95

TALK OF THE TOWN by Saxon Bennett. 239 pp. With enough beer, barbecue and B.S., anything is possible! ISBN 1-931513-18-X $12.95

MAYBE NEXT TIME by Karin Kallmaker. 256 pp. Sabrina has everything she ever wanted—except Jorie. ISBN 1-931513-26-0 $12.95

WHEN GOOD GIRLS GO BAD: A Motor City Thriller by Therese Szymanski. 230 pp. Brett, Randi, and Allie join forces to stop a serial killer. ISBN 1-931513-11-2 $12.95

A DAY TOO LONG: A Helen Black Mystery by Pat Welch. 328 pp. This time Helen's fate is in her own hands. ISBN 1-931513-22-8 $12.95

THE RED LINE OF YARMALD by Diana Rivers. 256 pp. The Hadra's only hope lies in a magical red line . . . climactic sequel to *Clouds of War*. ISBN 1-931513-23-6 $12.95

OUTSIDE THE FLOCK by Jackie Calhoun. 224 pp. Jo embraces her new love and life.
ISBN 1-931513-13-9 $12.95

LEGACY OF LOVE by Marianne K. Martin. 224 pp. Read the whole Sage Bristo story.
ISBN 1-931513-15-5 $12.95

STREET RULES: A Detective Franco Mystery by Baxter Clare. 304 pp. Gritty, fast-paced mystery with compelling Detective L.A. Franco ISBN 1-931513-14-7 $12.95

RECOGNITION FACTOR: 4th Denise Cleever Thriller by Claire McNab. 176 pp. Denise Cleever tracks a notorious terrorist to America. ISBN 1-931513-24-4 $12.95

NORA AND LIZ by Nancy Garden. 296 pp. Lesbian romance by the author of *Annie on My Mind*. ISBN 1931513-20-1 $12.95

MIDAS TOUCH by Frankie J. Jones. 208 pp. Sandra had everything but love.
ISBN 1-931513-21-X $12.95

BEYOND ALL REASON by Peggy J. Herring. 240 pp. A romance hotter than Texas.
ISBN 1-9513-25-2 $12.95

ACCIDENTAL MURDER: 14th Detective Inspector Carol Ashton Mystery by Claire McNab. 208 pp. Carol Ashton tracks an elusive killer. ISBN 1-931513-16-3 $12.95

SEEDS OF FIRE: Tunnel of Light Trilogy, Book 2 by Karin Kallmaker writing as Laura Adams. 274 pp. In Autumn's dreams no one is who they seem. ISBN 1-931513-19-8 $12.95